THE TRUTH ABOUT CINDER

ALTA HENSLEY

Thank you to Jay Aheer for the amazing cover! Also a big thanks
to Maggie Ryan for editing and helping my book turn to magic! I
also can't forget my amazing betas! You all know who you are,
and I love you. And of course all the readers that have supported
me along the way. I have the best team in the world.

To my daughters.
Always believe in the classic saying:
Once Upon A Time...
They Lived Happily Ever After.

1

Once Upon A Time...

The world dried up, leaving nothing but barren, infinite, monotonous desert. Desolate land with little vegetation except for the endless sagebrush and greasewood that spattered the horizon. No shade, nothing to offer refuge from the burning rays of the sun. Cinder stopped to listen to the deep, dead stillness of the sandy hills and valleys. No running water, no chirping of birds, no buzzing hum of life—not a single sound but her own ragged breathing. The desert had engulfed the globe.

The limitless sand ahead of her seemed to stretch to infinity. The enormity of the crossing became more and more obvious with every step she took. As Cinder plodded westward, doubt of survival congested her mind. Would she die before she reached her destination? Would the vast desert be her lonely grave?

She began the journey with as many provisions as she could carry, but she had no way of knowing if they would last. Collecting enough supplies in a commune, with very little to begin with, proved almost as difficult as trekking across the cruel wilderness to her destination. She was full of strength and fortitude, but was that enough to battle the ruthless land?

Nothing stood before her but the wasteland of the burning sands. She traveled days, weeks, she really wasn't sure anymore. Endless steps, agonizing climbs of ridged dunes that tormented every muscle in her body.

One step... two, was her mantra.

Cinder's core melted into the ground with every step. With her brown hair and sun-baked skin, she blended with the earth.

Brown, brown, brown—everywhere she looked —brown.

She marched forward hoping that any minute she would reach the Palace of Lazar. She'd soon see shimmering blue water, palm trees swaying in a delightful wafting breeze—the commune of dreams, and her ultimate destination.

The desert was made up of small communes

scattered throughout the world. Pods of civilization on small acres of precious, fertile land. For decades the people of this world survived off a wasteland of dried up lake beds, desiccated rivers and what little water the world still possessed. Communes formed around the few remaining water resources. Desert inhabitants lived in these communes, surviving off whatever resources the small community possessed—each commune being a tiny oasis overcrowded with people.

No one understood what had caused the massive disruption, but all suffered the consequences. Without water, civilization fell into anarchy. Droves of people combed the desert of death, seeking fertile land in the hopes of survival. Some communes thrived, while others eventually succumbed to the sun.

But no commune could measure to the Palace of Lazar. Some believed the palace was no more than a figment of the imagination. Nothing more than a fairytale told to children. But Cinder believed that this palace would soon be her home. This part of the desert was uncharted. Of all the explorers who had embarked this way before, none had ever returned to tell the tale of such a place.

But Cinder continued on.

She would make it, or die amongst the ones who'd tried.

By the time the sun plunged toward the horizon, her shadow became the only sign of life. It was a strange and unnerving feeling being so alone. Surviving in communes meant overcrowding. Everywhere she turned, someone would be there to meet her gaze. Shoulder to shoulder with strangers. The suffocating population of the communes caused many to flee in search of a better one. The desert nomads wandered the dried terrain in search of fertile land yet untouched by man.

Cinder was now among them—a lonely drifter with no home.

Walking alone in the endless, arid land, she watched the fading colors of the sun streak the sky with the palest gold to the richest reds. Magnificent hues reminded Cinder of the breathtaking space around her. A desert so deadly, but at times, so awe-inspiring.

The burning heat of the day dissipated a little, which allowed Cinder to pick up her pace. For days she'd camped at dusk, eaten a meager meal, and sipped at her treasured water supply before trying to sleep on her worn blanket. Now she had to change her routine. Cinder had used the last of her matches for fire lighting the night before, so stopping to make camp seemed pointless. When her hunger pains became unbearable, she ate what was left of her dried meat as she hiked forward.

Time was running out.

Stumbling over her own feet, Cinder had no choice but to stop for a quick rest. Exhaustion had won this battle. She was glad to spread her blanket down for a couple of hours' sleep.

Sweet dreams of the palace.

Sweet dreams of a prince who would swoop her up and save her from her harsh existence.

Sweet dreams of a fairytale.

Anything but the nightmare she was living now.

THE NEXT FEW hours passed all too quickly. The morning heat grew unbearable, burning through the blanket and making sleep impossible. Her lips were cracked and dry, her skin burned, and her eyes were gritty with sand. Struggling to lift her head, Cinder couldn't help but wonder if today would be the day she died. With her food now gone and only enough water to last the day, Cinder struggled to her feet to continue on. She would die fighting.

She concentrated on putting one foot in front of the other, one step at a time as she focused on breathing in and out in a soothing pattern. The need for water overwhelmed her until she had no choice but to take the last gulp she'd been attempting to save. As she took the final sip, she closed her eyes and tried to relish the pleasure of having something so cool against her tongue. If she were going to die, she wanted to remember the joy of something as simple as taking a drink.

She didn't want to die, but accepted that the outcome pointed in that direction. People had called her a fool for believing she could make this journey. Others questioned why she wanted to reach the palace to begin with. Stories of sex, lust, forbidden acts, and a society wrapped around taboo steered many away. The prince who ruled the commune was known for his insatiable tastes and the women who catered to it all. The Palace of Lazar was not just a commune.

It was a harem.

Unlike most communes, women were welcomed. Tales of jewels, satin, silk, and plentiful food drew the adventurous soul. But for Cinder, the palace offered more. The curiosity of what went on behind those walls pushed her through the desert day after day, night after night. The wonder of the harem and the prince haunted her dreams. Cinder wanted to see it, live it, and feel it.

It was worth risking her life and succumbing to the desert for even a chance.

The sand in front of her began to fade in and out. The ringing in her ears only intensified as her vision dimmed. She couldn't decide if she was going to faint or vomit, now convinced that her last moments were near. Everything started to recede as the darkness deepened until there was nothing but a hot, thick, encompassing, blackness.

2

She coughed frenziedly, gasping for air. The surprising coldness of something pushed hard against her lips, the action making her chapped skin crack even more in the corners of her mouth. She was vaguely aware that someone, or something, was trying to push liquid down her throat. As much as she wanted the cool fluid, her mouth and throat seemed to close shut. She realized that someone's finger pried her lips apart. She tried to open her eyes, but the weight of near death kept them shut. The trickling water down her throat seemed unreal.

Water.

She finally had water.

Someone was trying to make her drink water. She wasn't dead. She was indoors... somewhere.

Strident footsteps entered the room, stopping near her head. Cinder managed to slowly open her eyes and attempted to lift her body to a sitting position, failing miserably. Her blurred vision made it almost impossible to take in her surroundings. Colors—all she could see was an array of colors. She wiped at her eyes, trying to clear the sand from her travels as she tried to sit up again. A firm grasp on her shoulder pushed her back down.

There stood a man with eyes the color of the sea. Taller than most, dressed in all black, he exuded power. His shoulder-length, ebony hair merged with his collar. His superior appearance was flawless all the way to his meticulously groomed facial hair over his enticing mouth. His skin was so much darker than her own.

Mysterious, exotic, even frightening.

A deep, soothing voice boomed over her. "What is your name, girl?" His voice oozed with an intoxicating accent she hadn't heard before.

"Cinder." Her voice cracked, the dryness of her throat making it difficult to speak. She didn't recognize her raspy words.

"Cinder what? What is your last name?"

Cinder hated declaring her last name. It reminded her of her past. A past she tried so desperately to forget. "My name is Cinder Briar."

One of his eyebrows rose. "From the Briar commune?"

"Yes, sir."

Everyone's last name was the name of the commune in which they originated. It was a way to distinguish one's heritage. In Cinder's case, a heritage she wanted to forget.

"Briar Lake is a far journey. How did you get here?"

"I've lived in several communes since I left there. I've bounced from one failing one to another. I haven't inhabited Briar for over ten years in hope of finding... well, finding something better."

"Do you know where you are now?" he asked, taking a few steps so he stood directly in front of her.

"No, sir."

"You are inside the Palace of Lazar."

Cinder closed her eyes briefly as the very breath seemed to be knocked out of her. The overwhelming need to cry almost suffocated what air she had left. She had finally reached her destination. The desert wouldn't be her grave after all.

Was this real?

Had her fairytale finally come true?

The Palace of Lazar. She had finally arrived.

"Do you know what that is?"

"Yes, sir. I've been traveling for what feels like a lifetime to get here."

"For what reason?" His question was direct and sharp in tone.

"To be part of the harem." Saying the words out loud sent a quiver through her body. Maybe she shouldn't have been so direct, but she didn't know how to be anything but.

The corner of his mouth lifted into a small smile which disappeared as quickly as it came. He took a few steps closer to her. "You need to get some rest." His dark brow rose as his eyes narrowed to examine her tattered clothing and dehydrated body. "It took a lot of bravery to make the crossing here by yourself." He turned to leave the room.

"I didn't catch your name, sir?"

He glanced over his shoulder. "Donte. I am the person in charge of this harem. We'll discuss this further in the morning. Rest now." He paused to speak to a woman standing in the corner with the glass of water in her hand. "Clean her up, get her fresh clothing, and feed her some light broth. Her stomach won't accept food easily."

Even if Cinder had the strength to do so, she wouldn't dare argue with the man. His tone left her with no doubt that his orders were clearly expected to be followed without question.

THE SOUND of boots pounding against the marble slab of the room awoke Cinder from her sleep. She wasn't sure if she had dreamt it, or if she truly was inside the Palace of Lazar. A quick glance around proved her dream a reality.

Cinder watched Donte walk over to a round table with two chairs in the corner. He sat down without saying a word. The same woman who had cleaned and cared for Cinder the night before followed with a tray of tea and biscuits. She quickly left as soon as she placed the tray on the table.

"Good morning. I hope you slept well. Please come and join me." He motioned at the seat across from him.

Cinder stood up, slightly self-conscious of her appearance. She wore a white silk nightgown that covered the majority of her body. She had no doubt her hair was a mess, but there was nothing she could do about it at this point. Pulling the blankets back, she padded her bare feet across the floor to do as he asked. As she approached the chair, he stood and pulled it out for her. No one had ever done such a thing before.

Cinder stared at the austere man, intrigued. "Thank you."

He placed a biscuit on a plate, poured some tea

into a delicate cup, and set it in front of her. "Please, help yourself to the butter and jelly. There's sugar for the tea, if you like."

She gratefully accepted as her mouth watered. The spread before her was unlike anything she had ever experienced. She felt like a princess grabbing the sugar. She did the best she could to control herself as she reveled in the exquisite taste of the first real, solid food she'd eaten in days. Her hand shook as she brought the fine china cup to her lips. Although attempting to be graceful, Cinder knew she looked out of her element.

"If you want to be part of the harem, there are expectations," Donte stated in a businesslike tone. "You'll have to pass an inspection since we only accept virgins. After that, you'll have to go through extensive training. There are expectations and extremely high standards the harem will meet."

He leaned back in his lavishly carved chair. The dark wood table and chairs had men and women in sexual positions carved into the arms and legs. She couldn't keep her eyes from the delicate design. He noted her fascination.

"The wood was imported from a commune that harvests trees of all kinds. It is very rare, but endures well, and the artisan who created the furniture did an exquisite job, do you not agree?" He smoothed his palm over the armrest with a look of admiration and pride etched on his face. "I love when time is taken to make something perfect. Mediocrity should never be accepted. Craftsmanship is a dying art... much like our world today." His stormy blue eyes met Cinder's. "My expectations are high. In all regards."

She swallowed a bite of biscuit before speaking. "Yes, sir. I understand." Even though she said the words, she wasn't really sure she did, however. "I want to assure you that I am a virgin, and I'd be willing to go through whatever training you have in mind. I'm aware of what's expected."

His brow rose with interest. "You are?"

"I believe so. If I were part of the harem, my duties would be pleasuring the prince in any way he wishes. Though I have no experience, I'm willing to learn."

He smiled, continuing to rub his palm over the wood. Cinder noted his hands—big, capable, firm. Cinder needed to sip her tea to calm her growing nerves. She worried that if she came across too willing, he would think she was a woman of loose morals, but she also needed to make sure he was aware just how badly she wanted to be accepted. She was desperate and would beg if she had to.

"We have strict rules," he added, with a slight lift to his mouth. "You'll be expected to do as you're asked. In return, you'll be treated like royalty. If you disobey or act out, you'll be punished accordingly."

Cinder's heart skipped. "Punished? Like prison?" She didn't even want to think that death by execution would be an option here. She knew of many communes where torturous acts were performed on people every day where the victim ended up begging for death.

Donte gave a slight smile. "No, not prison. The girls of the harem are no strangers to severe discipline in a multitude of ways when deserved. But no prison, no permanent harm, and no death." He must have been reading her thoughts.

He paused, examining Cinder's face. She did everything she could to not appear shocked, concerned or upset by his statement. She wanted to appear sexually sophisticated, as well as worldly, even though she had no idea how to achieve it.

Donte continued on. "There are many versions of punishments, but all with the purpose to keep the harem submissive. Every man has different desires. Different cravings. But each one demands submission at some level."

"Submission?"

The image of being disciplined by Donte sent a shiver down her spine. Was it the idea of the punishment? The surrender of control? Or was it that having a discussion of this nature seemed so natural to the man?

"Yes. This will be part of the training. I have no doubt you'll truly understand the meaning soon enough."

"I see." She took another bite of the bread and swallowed. Donte's eyes watched intently as she chewed. "I'm a quick learner, and I promise you I won't let you down."

Donte crossed his arms against his broad chest. "What other communes have you lived in besides Briar?" His gray–blue eyes glinted with interest.

"I've been in many. Some I left by choice and others by force." Cinder glanced at her armrest where an exquisite carving depicted a couple engaged in a contorted sexual position. She couldn't help but wonder if she would someday partake in the same exact act. Her gaze snapped back to Donte. "The last commune was called Jaden. They were only interested in people who'd either be a warrior, or a bride to a warrior. I wasn't interested in either. The one before that only accepted potato pickers. The life seemed dreary and bleak. Communes are filling up, so the options are few."

"Warriors you say. Why do you think the commune Jaden wanted warriors? What is your take on that?"

Cinder stared at him, unable to speak at first. She'd never been asked her opinion on anything. "Fertile land is precious and extremely valuable. I think it's only human nature to want to have that land. Unfortunately, it's also human nature to fight for what you want. I think Jaden is planning on going to war with nearby communes. It's scary, really."

Donte nodded. "Do you have no family?"

His ability to jump from one topic to the next overwhelmed her. It was hard to keep her composure. Maybe that was his intent.

"No, sir." She looked down at the ground, praying he wouldn't press any further, or want more of an answer.

"It has been awhile since I've been beyond the palace walls. Is the land as parched as before?"

Stress released from her shoulders when she realized the conversation continued on. Cinder nodded. "Worse. It seems to be drying up more each day."

Donte studied her every move. His glare pierced through her. "Tell me of Jaden. You say they are accepting more people?"

Cinder nodded again. "One of the few communes that are. Since population controls have been set, very few communes allow new residents. Jaden is building its army." Her gaze went to another sexual carving in the wood. Speaking of the scorched world reminded her of how lucky she was to have made it to the Palace of Lazar.

"Why did you choose the palace?" His stare burned.

She smiled to try to hide just how uncomfortable his stare made her. "Anything's better than being a potato picker." She hadn't intended to be funny, but couldn't resist.

Donte chuckled. "Fair enough." He paused, and the short-lived smile melted away, leaving his serious, unyielding expression in its place. "No more talk of that." He slapped the desktop softly. "After you are done eating, we'll send you to be inspected. Training starts right after that. Do you have any questions?"

Cinder shook her head.

Donte sat in silence the rest of breakfast. He never took his eyes off of her. His face was stern as he studied her every move. "When you're through eating, please stand in front of me."

Cinder wiped her mouth with the cloth napkin and did as he asked. It was clear that Donte expected complete obedience of his every demand, and she wasn't about to question him or test his patience. She padded her way over until she stood only inches from him.

"Take off your nightgown."

The sharp command startled her, but she quickly did as he asked. She wasn't going to ruin her chance of food, water and shelter by allowing modesty to get in the way of what had been her long time goal. She unbuttoned the top buttons with shaky fingers, lifted the soft fabric above her head, and let the garment drop to the floor. She stood before him in nothing but white cotton panties that were given to her when she first arrived.

He rewarded her with a small smile. "I like that you did not pause or question. Very good."

Cinder smiled in return. She had traveled too far not to please him now. Her future rested in the hands of this man.

He stood and took hold of the elastic on the panties and lowered them down to her knees. He ran his fingers through the hair on her mound.

No, no, no. This was wrong. Sinful.

No man had ever touched her before.

Should she leave? Run out of the room and never look back?

No... this was the Palace of Lazar, and she knew what that meant. This is what she wanted. She'd had plenty of time during her journey to really ask herself if this was the life she wanted to live.

She had made her choice. Sinful or not.

Her choice was Lazar.

"After inspection, we'll send you to grooming. Body hair is not acceptable in the Palace of Lazar." He ran his index finger all the way down to her clit and pressed firmly. "I'm proud of you, Cinder. You have not flinched or pulled away from my touch. Most do until they are trained. I'm usually disappointed, but with you, I'm not."

Cinder swallowed the gasp threatening to escape, watching below hooded lids as he fondled her sex. His touch burned, tempting her to moan in desire. But Cinder stood silent, obediently allowing him to touch as he saw fit.

She was a soldier. A soldier of one. This was the way to win this battle. Stand at attention like a good soldier would.

He removed his hand and stared directly into her eyes. "You are a very good girl, Cinder." He walked toward the door and turned around. "There's a pair of fur slippers at the end of the bed. Place them on your feet. Remove your panties completely and follow me. It is time we make you part of the harem."

3

Completely naked, Cinder followed Donte down the hallway. She tried to keep pace with his long strides. The pattering of her fur-covered feet against the marble floor reminded her of her complete exposure with every step. Only her feet were covered... everything else on full display.

Donte looked over his shoulder and slowed his walk. His eyes scanned her unclothed body. "You'll learn to be comfortable eventually. As part of your training, you'll discover the beauty of your bare skin."

His firm, rumbling, baritone voice fired sparks in her core. A drop of arousal trickled down the inside of her leg. She pressed her thighs together to try to conceal what his voice alone had the power to do.

The anticipation of what was to come.

The unknown.

She should be terrified... but was anything but.

Now that they slowly walked down the hallway, Cinder could fully take in her surroundings. She noticed that every statue and piece of art featured portrayals of people engaged in various forms of sex. Tapestries hung from ceiling to floor, all with people in the most intimate positions. Vulgar angles, animalistic positions. So graphic, that Cinder felt her face heat and her nipples pebble while glancing at the visuals.

He followed her gaze to a painting on the wall. "Sex is beauty. Sex is art. You will be trained on how wondrous a sexual encounter can be. You'll soon be taught there is no shame in desire." The way he spoke mesmerized her, like a siren's song. "You will learn to not only expose your body freely, but your soul."

"Will you be doing the training?" Cinder recognized the hopeful undertones in her question. The thought of his tutoring caused tingling in her breasts. She glanced down at her nipples, hoping her thoughts weren't evident, but there was no hiding the fact.

"No. I will oversee it, but we have three mistresses highly skilled in the art of seduction and submission to provide the lessons. They are sisters who came to the palace in the beginning of its construction. Mistress Krin, Mistress Tula and Mistress Lana rule over the harem almost as much as I do, and I expect their dictates to be followed."

"I see." Cinder's cheeks grew warmer.

He chuckled quietly. The quick act surprised her. She had only seen this side of him briefly and found it odd how much it contrasted with the authoritative demeanor he possessed. "Let me show you the rest of the palace before we have you inspected and groomed."

After walking down several more hallways, he held out his hand, ushering her through another corridor. Cinder walked past him, still embarrassed that she was fully nude, yet her body hummed with every step she took. She caught an alluring trace of his spicy scent—dangerous, and so very masculine. Another bead of arousal formed between her legs. She hoped she wouldn't be this wet during the inspection. The lack of control of her bodily functions confused her.

Was it Donte? Was it the nudity? Was it the graphic décor cascading down every tapestry that covered every inch of wall space?

She was a virgin. Meant to be pure...

They walked until they reached a set of large

double doors. Intricate designs were sculpted into the wood just like the rest of the palace, but the doors also had jewels embedded into the carvings. The majestic door handle appeared to be etched from elephant tusk with tiny emeralds around the keyhole.

"We have reached the inspection room."

Cinder swallowed back her anxiety.

As if reading her mind, Donte added, "No need to be frightened."

She stared at him for a moment, taking in his assertive expression. She stood with anticipation of what came next.

"Cinder?"

His deep voice jarred her from her paralyzing thoughts.

"Shall we?"

Her body trembled as she walked ahead of him when he opened the door. She held her hands together in front of her and entered the room. The scent of olive oil and fresh poppies drifted through the air, giving notice that one of the windows was open to allow for the breeze. White curtains framed the scenery outside where a large cypress tree swayed in the wind. She could feel Donte's breath against her neck as he approached.

"Do not be afraid," he whispered.

On the first landing, Cinder noticed a petite

woman wearing a white dress. Although small, she exuded a superiority and confidence that Cinder had only seen in men. "You must be Cinder." She motioned to a table Cinder had seen once in a doctor's office. Doctors were rare, but when she almost died from the Tavarian flu a year ago, she was lucky enough to be in a commune that had one.

She stood in place, embarrassed that she was naked in front of another person. Donte placed his hand on Cinder's lower back and guided her to the exam table. "This is Mistress Krin. She is one of the three women who help oversee the harem. She'll be performing your examination."

Cinder's heart raced as she was led to the table. Donte gently assisted her, until she sat on the edge with her feet dangling free. On both sides of the table were metal foot holders. She almost gasped out loud when she realized she would be expected to put her feet in them. Her legs would be spread so wide. There was a small, metal tray, but Cinder couldn't see what was beneath the white cloth concealing its contents.

Mistress Krin approached the table and smiled. "Please take off your slippers and put your feet in the stirrups, push your bottom to the edge of the table, and lie back." The gentle tone of her voice soothed Cinder's bundle of nerves. She too had a thick accent, but it was somehow different from Donte's.

She quickly did as she was told, noticing that Donte stood behind Mistress Krin so he could observe all that was being done. Cinder tried to control the flush of heat spreading across her face as she spread her legs wide and stared at the ceiling. The sound of latex gloves being donned sent a shiver through her core. She closed her eyes and took a deep breath.

"You're going to feel something cold and then some pressure. Be a good girl and relax your legs. If you do as you are told, this inspection will be over in no time." Mistress Krin's gentle voice took on a bit more firmness this time around.

Before Cinder could take her next breath, something cold and metal entered her vagina.

"Just relax. The pressure will let up in a second," Mistress Krin soothed. "Lift your bottom up a little bit."

Cinder did as she asked, trying her best not to picture Donte watching her do all of this. Her legs were completely spread, and now her pussy was just as open.

"It is clear you're a virgin." Mistress Krin pulled out the metal device as she made the declaration. "I'm going to take your temperature now. Keep your legs wide."

Cinder gasped when she felt the tip of the thermometer against her anus. She jumped at the intrusion.

Mistress Krin gave a small swat to her pussy. "Stay still." The swat and the command sent a jolt of electricity through Cinder's entire sex.

The thermometer pressed against her hole again, but this time was inserted all the way in her anus. Mistress Krin left it firmly in place and walked around the table to examine her breasts. Her hands grabbed each one and massaged. She then pinched each nipple, causing Cinder to stifle a moan. Mistress Krin nodded in approval and walked back so she stood between Cinder's legs once again.

The thermometer was pulled out slowly. "No temperature. She also has plenty of sensation in her breasts and nipples." Mistress Kim grabbed a damp rag and wiped the lubrication off of Cinder's pussy and anus. "You can sit up now, Cinder."

She quickly did as ordered and instantly met Donte's approving gaze.

"Good girl. I'm pleased," he stated simply.

"Almost done, Cinder. Please roll over on to your stomach and spread your legs," Mistress Krin directed.

Cinder did as asked without delay.

"Lift your bottom up, and spread your legs wider."

Cinder spread her legs as wide as she could and pressed her bottom up and toward the ceiling. She had a pretty good guess as to what would be examined next and tried to calm her swelling nerves. It wouldn't end with just a thermometer.

"This part of the examination is going to hurt a little. I need to see how much your asshole can take. We need to see how much anal training is required for you."

Mistress Krin approached Cinder and pressed her lubricated finger to her exposed hole. She dipped her finger beyond the tight entrance and did this motion over and over, spreading the lubrication all around. Just the finger almost seemed too much to bear.

"It is important that you are honest with me, Cinder. Do you understand?"

Cinder nodded.

Mistress Krin swatted her butt. "From now on, when you are asked a question, you give a formal answer. Are we clear?"

"Yes, Mistress Krin."

"Even if it stings, you must accept what I put inside you until the sting turns to pain. Are we clear?"

"Yes, Mistress Krin."

"Do not cry out or ask me to stop until you absolutely cannot accept any more. Are we clear?"

Cinder nodded.

Mistress Krin quickly applied two hard spanks. "Are we clear?"

Cinder struggled for breath at the shocking bite of the swats. "Yes, Mistress Krin."

"I am going to start by inserting one of my fingers and then adding a second."

She did so, and Cinder tried her best to relax and breathe deeply. She knew if she cried out now, she would risk being told she wasn't ready to be part of the harem. Mistress Krin's fingers went in and out in small, slow thrusts. Cinder's pussy pulsated along with every push and pull.

"I am now going to put a small, slender dildo in. This may hurt, so you will need to calm down and allow the submissive sensations to take over."

Cinder wasn't exactly sure what a dildo was, but quickly felt it invade her backside. Cinder squealed as it pressed past her puckered entrance. Mistress Krin paused for a moment, but then continued to press it deeper within. Cinder wanted to cry out and beg for just the fingers again. She took deep breaths as instructed, but the sting became almost unbearable. Her bottom stretched to impossible limits as Mistress Krin pushed it all the way in. Cinder bit her lip and clenched at the edge of the table to quiet her ever building need to beg for mercy.

Mistress Krin reached between Cinder's legs and found her clit. She pressed firmly and rolled the tip of her finger in small circular motions. Cinder couldn't help but moan in pleasure and relax a bit.

"Allow the submission to set in. Relax and focus on submitting to the anal training. Know that with every stretch, you are getting closer and closer to where you can accept a cock in your ass. You'll be able to give the prince your ass for him to claim. It's a gift you can bestow. Submit, Cinder."

She did as commanded and allowed herself to feel something different. She couldn't explain the sensation, but it was as if all the fight had left her body. The dildo no longer seemed as foreign. It actually started to feel enjoyable. Cinder rocked her hips back and forth to match the circling of her clit. Heat radiated from her ass to her dripping wet pussy. Cinder wanted to explode. Lights sparked behind her closed eyes, and her body tingled everywhere. The pleasure grew with every thrust in her ass and every movement of Mistress Krin's finger. Cinder couldn't fight the urge to moan between her panting any longer. The sensation grew more and more until Cinder cried out. Mistress Krin sped up the thrusting, and applied more pressure to her clit, until Cinder's body tensed uncontrollably and fire shot through her. She let out a small scream as the foreign sensation racked her body over and over again. The pulsating in her pussy took her breath away.

Mistress Krin stopped what she was doing and removed the dildo. Cinder collapsed on the table, struggling to regain her composure.

"She's able to orgasm easily, although her ass will need daily stretching." She patted Cinder's behind. "Go ahead and sit up. The inspection is complete."

Cinder did as instructed, although her muscles felt like jelly. She looked into Donte's eyes and saw satisfaction and... arousal? That was her first orgasm, and she didn't know exactly what to think about it. Her mind swam, her heart pounded, and all she really wanted was to be comforted.

As if she had voiced her wants, Donte sat down on a large chair and patted his lap. "Come here, Cinder. You were a very good girl."

Cinder rushed over to him and sat on his lap. She didn't care that she was completely nude, or barely knew the man on whose lap she sat. Whatever had happened made her desperately want to be held. He wrapped his arms around her and rubbed her back as she nestled her head into his shoulder. His warmth, his whispered praise, his soft touch, made the journey across the unforgiving desert worth it. The Palace of Lazar would be her home. She nuzzled her face deeper into his neck and released a small whimper.

"Shhh... I could not have asked for more, Cinder. I think we found a gem in you."

4

"It's time we take you to get groomed." He lifted her off his lap, the heat of his body instantly missed.

She hesitated, wanting to close her heavy eyes and just feel safe in his arms. Safety was something she had never experienced... until now.

She reached down for her slippers but Donte stopped her. "Leave those here. We don't want the fur to get wet."

Cinder nodded and stood in place, unsure of what to do next. It felt like she needed to receive permission to do anything... even to take the ragged breaths she was taking.

"Go on, Cinder." He guided her through the door they had entered. "The palace consists of three levels and twenty-two bedrooms. The grounds are extensive, but you are forbidden to walk them unless permitted to do so, and only if escorted by someone. There are three pools and a cluster of five hot springs. You'll be spending most of your time in the central room with the other women of the harem," Donte explained as they walked down the hallway. "There are other wings of the palace, but you are only allowed to go there by invitation." He guided her to the right with his hand on her lower back. His fingers only mere inches from her naked bottom.

As Cinder walked down the corridor, her thoughts were overpowered by the grandeur of the ornately decorated hallway. The deep emerald-colored stones covering the tiled floor gave it a regal appearance, as if welcoming the footsteps of royalty. Elegant oil lamps provided light intermittently along both sides of the narrow hallway. At either end were two tall windows that reached from floor to ceiling. Tables flanked the walls of the corridor with statues of naked women and men placed on top.

He pressed his hand against her with a little more force as her pace had unintentionally slowed as she examined her surroundings. "There are guards patrolling the borders of the premises. I want you to feel comfortable knowing you are safe and well protected."

She nodded, offering him a brief smile. She didn't need guards. Cinder had never felt so safe in her life. This place was far different from the communes she was used to.

They continued down the hall. "Here we are." He opened the large double door, revealing a bath the size of a pool. Easily twenty people could bathe at the same time. Three crystal chandeliers hung above, catching the rays of the sun and painting shimmering rainbows along the walls. Cinder scanned the room and noticed several women standing off to the side, appearing to be awaiting their orders.

Donte led her over to the pool and helped her ease into the warm water. "Sit down." He motioned for one of the girls to approach. "We'll start by washing your hair."

Seeing so much water, let alone sitting in it, was a rarity greater than jewels. Engulfed in the magnificent waters, Cinder closed her eyes and released a soft moan. Heavenly.

The smell of jasmine filled her nose from the steaming water and a rich oil seeped into her skin as she sank as low as she could go, allowing the water to cover her shoulders.

"I feel like I'm in a dream." Cinder never opened her eyes in fear of waking up. The young girl washed her hair, scrubbing an eternity's worth of sand from her skull.

Cinder could have stayed in the bath for hours if it weren't for Donte's sharp command. "Stand and allow them to remove you of your body hair."

She blushed as she quickly followed his command. For some reason the act seemed more invasive than the inspection by Mistress Krin. Maybe it was that the hair displeased Donte, but Cinder couldn't help but feel some shame.

A dizzying sense of embarrassment assaulted her as another girl guided Cinder to spread her legs and began to shave the curly hairs off her mound. The girl took special care when she spread Cinder's pussy to remove the hair hidden by her silky folds. Cinder felt the need to snap her legs shut, but changed her mind the instant she glanced at Donte. He observed every move the young woman made, guaranteeing the job was performed to his level of satisfaction. One stroke at a time, the girl's delicate fingers fondled Cinder's sex. Once again, arousal rose from within. Cinder struggled to fight the sensation, self-conscious that an act of hygiene could stimulate such a reaction.

Painstaking moments passed by until Cinder stood, her body clean and completely bare, in front of Donte for inspection. Her long brown hair had been combed and lay like a curtain down to the middle of her back.

"Perfectly smooth," he said as he rubbed his fingertip over her hairless pussy. "This is what is required to be part of the harem. Any man would want to be able to observe your arousal. Men would want to see your juices, your engorged clit."

Cinder nodded, making direct eye contact. "Yes, sir." She couldn't keep the connection long and looked down at her feet.

He lifted her chin with a gentle nudge of his finger. "There's something different about you, Cinder. I've trained many women in this harem, but there is something that stands out with you. You are no ordinary woman."

She held his gaze, almost forgetting she stood before him nude until the breeze from the open window brushed across her damp skin.

"I think you'll fit into the harem seamlessly. But are you positive this is something you truly wish for?"

"Yes," she replied, captured by his sensual eyes. They were like a drug to her. "I've traveled a long way and for an even longer time to fulfill my dream of finding this fairytale."

He nodded as he pulled her hair forward with both of his hands, allowing it to tumble over her shoulders. The hair barely touched her nipples. Such a simple act, yet it sent an intense rush of emotion through her body. Nerves swept over her as Cinder wondered what was next. Would the training begin?

His hand slid over her hardened nipple, resting just beneath the curve of her breast. His movements were so controlled, so entitled, so powerful. "You don't flinch at my touch. You don't struggle with my command. All I see is arousal. Why is that, Cinder?"

"I don't kn... know," she stammered. Filled with desire, Cinder struggled for air. If he could read her thoughts, she wondered if his hands would work their way down to her hungry sex like she craved. She was greedy for another orgasm like Mistress Krin had given her.

"I see that today has awakened your sexual appetite," he said, reading her thoughts as his hand cupped the searing flesh between her legs. Cinder remained still, even though she wanted to rub against his hand, fueling another orgasm from her ravenous body.

"I think I've always had the appetite. I just had no way to feed it," Cinder whispered, hoarse.

She sighed as his thumb brushed across her clit and then pulled away completely. He teased her to the point of begging. What would he think if she did?

"You truly are a gem, my dear Cinder. I'm pleased." He moved a wayward hair from Cinder's forehead and examined her eyes. "You look tired."

Cinder nodded. Exhaustion caused her legs to feel weak and unstable, not to mention the sexual heat pulsating through her veins.

"I can see you're not fully recovered from your desert crossing."

Cinder nodded again. She didn't want to appear fragile or even lazy, but lying would be futile.

"I'm going to take you back to a private room for the night. Tomorrow you can meet the rest of the harem. Tonight you rest."

Cinder wasn't going to argue. Sleeping in a bed with pillows and blankets sounded almost as heavenly as the bath she'd just enjoyed.

In a lust-filled fog, she walked with Donte down another hallway. The need for sexual fulfillment titillated her very core, yet she wanted nothing more than to lie on the luxurious bed and dream of her future.

Donte opened the bedroom door and waited for her to walk past him. "Rest now. Be sure to eat all your meals. You'll need your strength. I'll be back in the morning."

Cinder barely had enough strength to nod. "Yes, sir."

"You did well today. I'm glad you chose to make the journey." He closed the door behind him quietly.

5

Cinder stood staring out the window, the breeze causing the sheer-white curtain to dance around her body. She had been up for over an hour waiting for Donte's return. Breakfast had already been brought to her, and now she had nothing to do but anxiously wait. She decided to remain nude since that was how he wanted her yesterday.

Looking through the glass, it amazed her how it was impossible to see any signs of desert from where she stood. The groundskeepers did an impeccable job of creating a lush and green landscape. Most communes were lucky for a few trees, let alone manicured grass. An array of birds chirping fascinated her. Some were low in pitch, others called out in a rapid staccato—songs of love, whistles that beckoned one mate to the other. How many varieties existed here? From just listening, it sounded like hundreds. Birds were merely a food source in all the communes of her past. They were not signs of beauty as they were in the Palace of Lazar. What an extraordinary and delightful sound.

A firm knock, followed by Donte entering the room, snapped Cinder out of her thoughts. She turned, greeting him with a welcoming smile.

"Good morning. I trust you slept well," he said as he walked to where she stood.

"I did. I'll forever be grateful for your hospitality." Surprised that she had no embarrassment standing nude before him, she stiffened her spine a little more in pride.

"I apologize for being late. I had some security issues I had to address." He stood beside her and looked out the window. He remained there a moment, silent, as he stared out. "Do you have any questions now that you have had a night's rest and time to think?"

"When will I be part of the harem. To serve the prince?"

Donte merely glanced over his shoulder. "When you're ready. When you're invited. There are many women in the harem who have yet to put their skills to service. In the meantime, you'll be trained and prepared so if called, you'll be ready."

Donte seemed different than yesterday. His thoughts seemed far off. As he stared out the window, it appeared as if worry washed over his face.

After a long moment of silence, Cinder whispered, "Donte? Is everything all right?"

He snapped out of his lost thoughts instantly. "Yes." He blinked clarity back into his eyes and asked, "Did you eat all of your breakfast?"

Cinder nodded. "Yes, sir."

Donte glanced over her shoulder to the unfinished plate of food. "How is that? I still see half of your meal on the plate." His distant glare soon replaced with authority.

Cinder followed his gaze to the breakfast dish and clarified. "I meant that I was finished eating breakfast. I guess I'm not used to the large amount of food."

Donte gave a quick nod. "I understand that. But when I told you to eat all your meals, I was not asking. I was telling." He walked over to the table, pulled out the chair, and sat.

Cinder wrung her hands in front of her nude body. "I'm sorry. I'll make sure not to waste again."

Donte gave another quick nod. "Yes, you will."

He glared at her firmly. "Come over here and lay across my knee."

Cinder almost gasped but didn't want Donte questioning if she was right for the harem. Her heart beat so hard it actually hurt. She didn't hesitate, but every step seemed as if she were walking through quicksand. She had a pretty good idea what he intended to do. Discipline? Was he actually going to punish her as he had threatened he would do? Had she displeased him so much?

She stood before him and did as he asked without being told again. She would never question Donte, for he held her future in his hands. The cotton of his pants, the firmness of his thighs, the short distance from her nose to the ground, all reminded her of the precarious position she was in.

"Once again, you surprise me, Cinder. You did not resist my order. Because of that, I'll not spank you for as long, or as hard, as I was intending to."

Before she could reply, a stinging swat to her behind took her by surprise. She couldn't help but gasp. Another swat, then another, and another.

"The three mistresses and I are strict with the harem, or they will rule us instead of us ruling them. When I tell you to do something, whether it is a command or a request, you are to do exactly as

I say. Regardless of how simple or minor that request is."

Her whole body jumped when his palm cracked across her bottom. She could feel the breadth of his palm, the stretch of his fingers—his hand was so large it nearly covered both her cheeks entirely and imparted such a sting that try though she did to hold herself obedient and still, there was just no way.

"You traveled a great distance to get here."

His spanking as ruthless as his scolding, he slapped her bottom again and her legs kicked, an involuntary jerk that snapped her feet up off the floor and sent shockwaves radiating through her flanks.

"You almost died on your journey here."

As the spanking continued, heat bloomed under her skin, inflaming everywhere his hard and capable hand met her flesh. "I don't want you spending your first few days in the infirmary. It's important that you take your health seriously."

He continued to pepper her backside rapidly. Cinder did her best to squeeze her eyes shut, clench her teeth, and take the punishment like a good harem girl would do... or what she would assume a harem girl would do. But after the tenth spank, she couldn't help but yelp and wiggle with each continued slap. Her backside reminded her of the hot sands of the desert she had just crossed.

Just as she thought she couldn't take it any longer, and was about to scream for mercy, he stopped the spanking.

"Stand up. The punishment is done."

She quickly stood, feeling a little dizzy at first. She wanted to rub her bottom, but thought better of it. He hadn't give her permission or a directive to do anything but stand up. Donte's expression made it clear he meant business.

He stood up and gently placed a fingertip between the folds of her pussy. Removing his moist finger, he smiled in satisfaction. "Your arousal pleases me."

The heat burning Cinder's face almost matched the heat on her ass. She couldn't resist looking down at her feet. She could hear him walk over to one of the ornately carved dressers. She glanced up in curiosity. He pulled out a long piece of silk fabric the color of the sunset.

"Go ahead and put this sarong on. At times you will be expected to be nude, and at times you will not. For now, you may get dressed."

Cinder reached for the fabric, unsure what to do with it. There were no holes or buttons. Feeling Donte's stare, she quickly decided to wrap it around her like a bath towel and tucked it in at the top.

Donte chuckled. "Here, let me help you." He twisted the material a few times, and expertly draped it around her body. "The girls of the harem will help you with the different ways you can wear this, but for now, I think this will do."

She turned so she was looking in the mirror. Donte had somehow made her look like she was wearing an exceptional custom tailored gown. "I can't believe you did this. It's so beautiful."

He placed his hand on her lower back, as he had yesterday, and ushered her toward the door. "It is time we introduce you to the harem."

6

Dressed in silks and satins of lovely shades, the women of the harem stood as Cinder and Donte walked into the room. Intricate hanging lanterns casting prisms of light in all directions were strewn along the twelve-foot-arched ceilings. Crystals hung between each, creating an illusion of enchantment and mysticism. Colors, beauty, grandeur, and luxury were only a few words Cinder could think of to describe this room. Lush pillows scattered about the floor. Tapestries meshed with the woven rugs that blanketed the white marble flooring. Gold glitter danced in the air, resting on the delicate skin of the women. A metallic chime near the open window tinkled a captivating melody.

"Ladies, I would like to introduce our newest

member of the harem, Cinder. I have no doubt that you'll welcome her and make her feel at home." The end of Donte's statement came out as a warning rather than a statement.

Cinder wanted to hide behind Donte. She didn't want to be stared at by everyone. What would they think? Would they welcome her? She scanned the beautiful women and noticed that all seemed interested. A young woman, with beautiful blonde hair, stared at Cinder with huge blue eyes. She smiled and nodded the minute Cinder made eye contact. The reassurance wasn't something Cinder thought she needed until now.

"Perfect timing, we were just about to begin today's anal training," Mistress Krin stated flatly. Cinder watched the pretty blonde wince at the statement, and wondered if she herself should be concerned. All she could remember was how Mistress Krin issued her first orgasm. The idea of anal training sounded exciting if it meant having another one.

"Then I'll leave you be," Donte said. Cinder glanced over her shoulder and met Donte's steely gaze. "It's expected that you follow every command any of the Mistresses give you."

Cinder nodded. "Yes, sir." She went and stood beside the pretty blonde when Donte motioned for her to do so.

"You're really pretty," the blonde girl whispered. "My name's Elbi."

From behind, Mistress Krin issued a warning with a steady, quiet tone. "Silence, Elbi."

"Sorry, Mistress Krin," the girl stammered.

"Perhaps I should show Cinder what happens when rules are broken," Mistress Krin suggested.

"That won't be—" Cinder began, but Donte's hand touched her lower back with a firm warning. There was something about Elbi that made Cinder want to stand up for her.

"I expect you to behave, Cinder. I hope I'm not called to address any behavioral issues." He pressed her lower back a little firmer and turned to walk out of the room. He paused and looked over his shoulder. "Cinder is not familiar with the rules of the harem. I expect you ladies to offer your advice and guidance. For the first week she's here, if she gets in trouble, you all get in trouble." Cinder felt the weight of the world on her shoulders as she watched him exit and close the door.

"Elbi," Mistress Krin continued, "I think we can start the training off with you. The rest of you ladies can introduce yourselves to Cinder."

Visibly bashful, Elbi's round cheeks blushed. She followed Mistress Krin to a long, slender, cherry-wood table. Without being asked, she lifted her pink-tinted silk sarong, exposing her nude bottom, and bent over the table.

"I'm Maysa," another pretty girl said, snapping Cinder's attention from watching Elbi wait for her training. Maysa smiled warmly. "Don't worry, by the end of the week you'll feel right at home. It takes a few days, but you'll love it."

The next few moments were a blur of introductions. Cinder did her best to memorize all the names, but the flurry of female attention overwhelmed her. The hushed chatter of women buzzed in her ears.

She leaned in and whispered to Maysa, "What is anal training?"

She shrugged. "It's different for each person. But basically, it's getting your anus ready for a cock."

Cinder's mouth dropped in shock. Would she be expected to do all of this in the full view of others?

"Don't look so shocked." Maysa giggled. "You better get over being inhibited real quick here. There's no privacy and no secrets in this harem. Even if you tried."

The rest of the women went back to their business and conversations as if Cinder was already ancient news. Maysa remained sitting beside her.

A loud slap, followed by a squeal, pulled Cinder's attention back to Elbi bent over the table. Mistress Krin was spanking her with a wooden paddle that was intricately carved like all the furniture in the palace.

"Is that part of the anal training? The wooden paddle?" Cinder asked, trepidation causing her voice to crack.

Maysa glanced over her shoulder with little concern. Apparently seeing another woman get hit with wood was of no surprise to her. "Oh, Elbi's been cheating. She doesn't like wearing her plug and has been sneaking it out. Mistress Krin noticed her tight hole isn't ready for the prince if he were to request her. So now she's getting punished."

"How would she know?" Cinder had no idea what Maysa was speaking of. How exactly would one be *ready* for the prince?

Cinder watched as the paddle cracked against Elbi's red behind over and over. The pretty woman cried out as she wiggled her ass in an attempt to avoid each blow. Cinder didn't want to ask further questions about Elbi in fear of how naïve it would make her sound, but there were so many questions flooding her mind that she wasn't able to help herself.

Cinder took a deep breath, attempting to extinguish the electricity buzzing in her veins.

"Does Mistress Krin do all the training?" She glanced over her shoulder and watched as Mistress Krin continued to spank Elbi. Watching the act made her stomach flip and her sex pulse for an unknown reason. Why would seeing a woman's distress do such a thing?

"I wish. She's the easiest. There are two more but the worst is Mistress Tula," Maysa replied.

"What about Donte?" Just saying his name caused Cinder to miss his presence.

Maysa shook her head. "You do *not* want Donte to punish you. Trust me."

"Why?"

Maysa smiled. "You'll see for yourself. But I'd much rather feel the sting of anyone's hand but his."

Cinder almost shared that she had already been corrected by him, but decided to keep the information to herself. From the sound of it, Donte must have been pretty easy on her.

Mistress Krin requested another woman of the harem to come join her as Elbi made her way back to where Cinder and Maysa sat. She eased her way down slowly, struggling to find a comfortable way to place her spanked and plugged bottom on the pillows. She winced as she sat.

Maysa shook her head. "You did this to yourself."

"Quiet. I wasn't asking for your opinion," Elbi said as she stuck her tongue out.

Maysa chuckled.

"So not fair!" Elbi whispered. "The plug is two sizes larger than the one I wore yesterday."

Cinder looked at Maysa for explanation. Plug?

Maysa smiled. "You'll see what a plug is in a few moments." She looked at Elbi. "Well, try not to take this one out. You make it harder on yourself."

"I hate the plug. It bothers me," she pouted. "I'd rather get a spanking."

Cinder found Elbi's honesty refreshing, if not endearing. "Do we have to wear a plug every day?" Cinder asked.

"No," Maysa said. "There isn't a strong routine here. We just do as we're told. Some days there is training. Some days there are punishments. Some days there are rewards."

Elbi crossed her arms against her chest, continuing her pout. "I want a reward." She adjusted her body again, grimacing as she did so. "This plug is too big. I hate it," she whined.

Mistress Krin called out another name, and then another. Each lady of the harem rose with poise and refinement and made her way to the table. Cinder sat anxiously waiting for her name to be called. When it finally was, Cinder's heart stopped.

She took slow steps toward Mistress Krin, each one being used to build her courage. Fear mixed with curiosity almost numbed her senses.

As a woman of the harem, her turn had come.

She had to keep telling herself that this is what she had wanted. This was what she had traveled across a ruined landscape to reach.

She lifted the smooth material of her wrap, and at the same time, lowered herself across the table as she had watched all the women before her do. Feeling the cool air against her upturned bottom sent shivers across her skin.

"Spread your legs." The command wasn't harsh, just simple.

Cinder did as ordered.

"Since you're new, we'll start with a small one." Mistress Krin reached around with the plug in her hand so Cinder could see what it looked like. It was metal, and a small purple stone sat at the base. Cinder found it odd that something so beautiful would be planted in her backside.

Cinder could hear Mistress Krin put on a pair of latex gloves. Mere seconds later, a moist finger inserted its way past her tight opening. No warning was given, just a finger smearing a form of lubrication all around. Before Cinder could come to terms with the finger in her hole, it was replaced by the tip of the metal plug.

"Relax," was all she heard as the plug pushed past her tight anus.

A gasp, a clench at the edge of the table, were the only things Cinder could focus on. A biting pain, mixed with erotic fascination had her pussy beckoning for more. It hurt at first. Hurt more than Cinder had remembered from yesterday, but with every breath she took, the pain turned to a heated pulse in her core. The throbbing teased her need for more. The sting strummed at her lust.

With a slight pat on her bottom, Mistress Krin broke the sexual spell. "You're finished. Go ahead and join the other ladies."

Cinder stood up and lowered her clothing to cover her invaded ass. With every step toward Maysa and Elbi, Cinder could feel the weight of the plug. Her sexual desire growing with every move she made, Cinder wondered if the women could read her ravenous thoughts.

When she sat down next to Maysa, she understood why it had taken Elbi a few moments to get comfortable. Applying pressure to the base of the plug only made the intrusion more obvious. Cinder actually considered standing, but didn't want to single herself out as different.

"Wait until you get to the size she put in me," Elbi whispered. "You'll want to sneak it out, too."

Cinder smiled. She liked the devious sparkle in Elbi's eye.

Anal training had begun. Cinder now stood as a lady of the harem.

This is what she wanted.

Her fairytale...

7

Months had passed filled with a leisure unfamiliar to Cinder. Hours of the day were occupied with relaxation, idle chat, and a sense of sisterhood she hadn't expected. When the harem were not being groomed or trained, they were left to flourish as women. Extracurricular activities were encouraged. Voice lessons, sewing, reading, and writing were only a few of the hobbies offered. Cinder had decided to learn how to play the guitar. Her instructor spent several hours a day teaching her the ways of the flamenco—music that originated in southern Spain many centuries ago. Something about the historical romanticism pulled at her soul. The way her fingers plucked at the strings, how the shape of the instrument reminded her of the female body, and the way the sound filled a room, hypnotized her. Everything about the instrument called to her, everything except the actual lessons themselves. She dreaded her next one, awaiting the wrath of Mistress Tula.

"No, that is not how that works!" Mistress Tula shrieked as the lesson continued. Her accent sounded very similar to Donte's.

Cinder cringed as her instructor picked up her foot and slammed it down on the marble floor, making a slapping sound that echoed in the huge room. Cinder sat back in her chair, holding her guitar close to her body. She wanted to ask why it didn't work, but she didn't want her to grow any angrier.

Her instructor, Mistress Tula, was skilled in the art of flamenco guitar, but at this point, she seemed to only be bullying her around instead of actually teaching her. In fact, Mistress Tula hadn't picked up a guitar once since Cinder's session started an hour ago.

Mistress Tula paced back and forth in front of her, muttering something under her breath. She wasn't much older than Cinder, and her young, smooth skin crinkled as she furrowed her brow with frustration. Her dark hair was pulled in a loose braid, some of it falling into her piercing eyes. While Cinder herself was barely 5-foot-2, Mistress Tula stood at a lofty 5-foot-10.

"I'm sorry," Cinder said in a quiet voice. She hated knowing Mistress Tula was disappointed or angry with her. It was the same with any of the training performed at the harem. In her mind, the harem had given her so much, and when she didn't excel at something, she felt ashamed.

Mistress Tula whipped around to face her. "You're *sorry*? Again, that is not how this works. You do not *apologize* in music. You make your statement with music and do not look back. Music is not an apology. It is the blood flowing in any musician's veins. Now, play that segment again and this time, do not be sorry."

Cinder broke eye contact with her, feeling the hairs on the back of her neck prickle. She raised her hand and launched into the segment of music, her body moving gently with the beat she devised.

She loved the sound of the music more than anything, and loved that she chose it as her extra-curricular activity at the harem, but what Cinder hadn't known was how difficult her instructor was going to be on her. Mistress Tula was ruthless, often stopping Cinder in the middle of a piece or even after only a few seconds of playing. Sometimes, she wouldn't let her start playing until

Cinder achieved the perfect posture, and because Mistress Tula wasn't satisfied easily, that could take up an entire lesson.

But even while Mistress Tula was a strict disciplinarian to her in lessons, Cinder found herself taking a liking to her. There was something about the way she moved, the way her eyes seemed to see into Cinder's soul. She could see and understand the way the music put her in a trance.

"Stop, stop, stop," Mistress Tula shouted, waving her hands.

Cinder immediately cut off, her eyes growing wide. "What did I do wrong this time?" she asked, surprised at how bold her voice sounded. In her lessons, it was always, "What did I do wrong?" not "What did I do right?"

Mistress Tula stared at her with a cold gaze. "First of all, a six-year-old's posture is better than yours right now. You have got to sit up properly and grip the guitar correctly, or else you will not play this music as it should be played. You are not giving it justice. Respect the music."

Cinder gritted her teeth together to keep from snapping back at her. She was always so harsh on her, and Cinder expected the world to end before Mistress Tula ever gave her somewhat of a compliment.

"Second of all, you missed several notes," she went on as she began pacing again. Her favorite thing to do during Cinder's lesson was pace; she hardly ever took a moment to sit down in her chair.

Cinder let her shoulders slump as she listened to Mistress Tula list her flaws and mistakes. At this point, she hardly took offense to them. The woman had constantly insulted her and her playing ever since she started lessons, so she had grown accustomed to it.

"Now, are you ready to start playing again?" she asked.

Cinder nodded mutely.

"What are you waiting for?" Mistress Tula demanded. "Start playing!"

Cinder brought her shaking hands up to the guitar and carefully picked at the strings, fumbling through a line of notes and rhythms. With each note she missed or rhythm she messed up, she cringed and knew anger was probably bubbling up under her instructor's skin.

"Stop," Mistress Tula moaned, grabbing her head with her hands. "What are you doing? You have been taking lessons with me for a while now and you *still* play like a beginner. My other beginners could probably show you up if they were here right now."

Cinder sat there, a lump lodged in her throat. All she did was look forward. If she looked at her instructor, Cinder knew she would end up bursting into tears.

Mistress Tula demanded that she start playing again, making sure she got the notes and rhythms right. She jumped back into the music.

Normally, playing this kind of music would have set her soul free, and every time she practiced it did, but with Mistress Tula, it felt like she couldn't express herself at all. It felt like Mistress Tula was expressing *her* vision through Cinder's hands.

For the next hour, it was a trial and error process. Every time she missed a note or rhythm, Mistress Tula snapped at her or forced her to play that measure over again. With each insult she threw at her, Cinder became more and more unstable, the urge to quit lessons growing stronger —if that were even a possibility.

For the fifteenth time, Mistress Tula stopped her and forced her to play a certain section over again.

"Are you ready to start playing like an intermediate student?" she demanded.

"Are you ready to stop insulting me?" Cinder snapped, but gasped instantly after the words passed her lips. They had been bubbling on the tip of her tongue and had just come out without her having control over them. Her heart stuttered... recognizing she was in trouble.

Even without looking at Mistress Tula, she knew that the woman had stopped pacing and was glaring at her with her delicate hands folded behind her back.

"What did you say?" Mistress Tula asked slowly, making the hairs on the back of Cinder's neck prickle.

Finally, Cinder looked at her and made eye contact, even though she wanted to run straight out of the large room.

"I'm ready to start being treated as a musician," she said slowly, her voice shaking a little. "Battering me with all the insults I've already heard before won't make me any better." *What was she doing? Did she want to be disciplined?*

Mistress Tula leaned back on the heels of her feet and glanced up at the ceiling. "You are a feisty one, and very, very foolish." With a fluid motion of her hand, she pointed to the corner in the far right of the room. "Go kneel with your nose in the corner. Now!"

Cinder gently placed her guitar in the open case, and stood on shaking legs. She made her way to the corner, trying not to look at Mistress

Tula standing with her arms crossed against her chest.

"When you reach the corner, remove your silks," she ordered. "I'll go fetch Donte to issue your discipline. Do not move an inch."

Cinder did as she was told without hesitation. She was in enough trouble as it was. The idea of Donte coming sent a panic through her. What would he do? She hadn't been corrected by his hand since that first time when she arrived at the palace, and the idea of being punished again sent a terrifying shiver up her spine.

Her body trembled as she stared at the corner of the wall, listening closely to any sound. The wait was agonizing. Kneeling nude, in punishment, made her feel extremely vulnerable and tears threatened to fall. She didn't want to disappoint Donte. She kneeled long enough that her legs grew tired of the bent position. She adjusted her weight from one thigh to the other, fidgeting with her hands out of nervous energy. Just as she thought she would go mad kneeling there, she heard footsteps behind her. The heavy sound of boots hitting marble made it clear that Donte had entered the room.

"Cinder," his voice sliced through the silent air.

"Yes, sir." She closed her eyes and tried to steady her breathing. She remained facing the corner.

"Mistress Tula informs me that you have been disrespectful. Is this true?"

"Yes, sir." She didn't truly believe the words, but arguing would only make it worse.

"Please turn around and face me."

Cinder did as he asked and stood with her hands placed in front of her body. The fact that she stood nude before him, about to be disciplined, caused her lip to quiver. She quickly bit it to try to conceal her fear. She stared at the ground so she wouldn't have to look at his and Mistress Tula's glares.

"Mistress Tula," he said, "please leave me alone with Cinder."

The much softer sound of footsteps receding told Cinder her instructor was leaving the room without saying a word.

When the door clicked shut, Cinder lifted her gaze enough to see Donte walk over to a chair and sit down. He patted his thigh. "Come here."

Cinder had to will her body to move toward her impending doom. Step after step, she inched her way toward him. She stood before him and made eye contact.

He patted his lap again. "Sit on my lap."

She paused, taken aback that he didn't ask her to lie across it. She sat on his lap as he commanded, unsure of what was going to happen next.

"Do you feel you deserve a punishment? I want the truth."

Cinder took a deep breath. "No, sir. I don't believe I do."

"Why is that?"

"I was just speaking my mind," Cinder muttered. "Mistress Tula can be... infuriating during a lesson."

Donte nodded. "She is firm. She demands perfection."

"Yes, sir. I try my best. I do. I practice for hours every day." Her lip began to quiver again. "But sometimes I don't feel as if this is the right fit for me. I don't feel as if I will ever be as talented as the other women in the harem. They have a level of sophistication I don't have."

"I disagree," he stated firmly. "I feel you are the perfect fit. I wouldn't have allowed you into the palace if I didn't feel that way."

Cinder looked down at the ground as his words caused a warmth to run through her.

"I want you to play for me," he commanded softly.

She stood from his lap and made her way to her guitar. Without another word, she launched into the song, her fingers working expertly on the strings. She continued to play, never looking at Donte. She just played, and played, and played, letting the music fill her body and tingle the tips of her fingers.

She played until the room was filled with the harmonious notes of the guitar and for once, it actually sounded good to her. When she reached the end of the song, she stopped and the music echoed against the walls and high ceiling.

When the music faded, all Cinder could hear was the sound of her pulse rushing in her ears. She knew that Donte had watched her every move, but she didn't pay attention to that fact. Nor the fact that she played completely nude.

"That was beautiful," he said quietly. "It's a shame that our world has very few people who know how to play an instrument anymore. I love seeing your take on the guitar. It's one of my favorites."

Cinder snapped her head to the side to look at him and found his eyes and expression soft. "Really?"

"You have never looked more beautiful," he added, making Cinder blush at the compliment.

"I want to hear another song. I want you to approach this piece with fire in your heart and ice on your mind. You need to have passion, but you also need to focus and concentrate. I can see you get lost in the music, but then you lose focus on the skill. No doubt Mistress Tula's frustration."

Cinder nodded as she started to look over the sheet music of a piece she had been practicing relentlessly, fingering each note as she came across it. She couldn't help but feel Donte's burning gaze sear on her skin and her hands grew a little shaky.

Donte rose from his chair, moving behind her. He gently placed his hands over hers and Cinder wanted to jump back. His hands felt like fire burning the backs of her hands. He leaned forward, their faces inches apart, and Cinder did everything to keep from turning her head to look at him.

Carefully, Donte guided her hands over the correct notes and held them steady, plucking out the notes to the rest of the song. When they reached the end, he stood back and returned to his chair, leaving Cinder in a daze. All she could focus on was the thick aroma of his essence.

"Now you try," he prompted, nodding at her.

Cinder chewed on her lower lip, but launched into the song slowly, picking at the notes and fumbling in a few places. As she progressed through the song, making mistake after mistake, she wondered if he would yell at her like Mistress Tula.

Finally, she reached the end of the piece and

sat back, the tears already burning the backs of her eyes. She awaited his outburst.

But nothing harsh came from his mouth. All he did was lean forward to rest his elbows on his knees and say, "Very nice. It is rough around the edges, but with polish you'll have a jewel. You've come a long way in a very short time."

Cinder blinked, hoping he wouldn't notice the tears of gratitude in her eyes, and she let out a long breath. "You think so?"

"I see your love," he said with a warm smile. "I can see how the music enters your body and gives you a light in your shadowed eyes. I have wondered what caused such darkness. Maybe you'll share with me sometime."

Cinder stared at the ground. The intimate softness of his voice unnerved her.

"I'm not going to discipline you today," he declared. "But you would be wise to not speak to Mistress Tula in any way but with respect."

Cinder sighed in relief. "Yes, sir. It won't happen again."

"No, it will not." He stood up and made his way toward where Cinder sat. "From now on, you'll have your lessons with me. I would hate for Mistress Tula's method of teaching to extinguish any of the love I see." He moved a piece of her hair off her shoulder. "That is enough for today."

Cinder nodded and packed up her instrument, sliding it into the case and grabbing her sheet music. Awkwardly, she rose and nodded to him. "Thank you, sir. I would enjoy that."

Donte barely smiled, and it was enough to send the heat rushing to her face. "I will see you in a few days, Cinder."

With that, Cinder practically ran out of the large room. As soon as the door shut behind her, she allowed herself to take a few gasping breaths. Setting her case and music down, she held her hands up in front of her to see them shaking a bit, and she clasped them firmly together to ease the tremble. Finally, she leaned against the wall, grinning in pure happiness.

Donte captured her breath, her heart, her soul. There was something about his dark eyes that sent her swooning, and his voice was deep and methodical.

"Cinder..."

She whipped around to see Donte standing in the doorway with his hand out. "You forgot your silk."

Her eyes widened, embarrassed. She rushed to meet him and took her clothing from his hand. "Thank you."

"I'll see you soon," he said as he retreated toward the room.

For a moment, all Cinder could do was nod.

"Yes, of course," she finally said. A small smile pulled at the corner of his lips as he shut the door.

She quickly dressed, took a calming breath to steady her nerves, and grabbing her belongings, stumbled down the hallway to join the harem, grateful she didn't have a sore backside and the blush of shame as she did so.

8

The culture, the friendship, and the bonds became her new way of life. As much as her life had become a dream, she still longed for the sexual touch of a man. Her curiosity to meet with the prince consumed her thoughts. She couldn't help but wish to please, to submit, to succumb to the sexual pleasures. But more than anything, her thoughts always found their way back to Donte and her next lesson. Anything to be near him. It didn't help that her body remained in a constant sexual haze from all the training. Anal plugs became a way of life. Masturbation wasn't allowed, but many snuck the release regardless. Cinder still feared the carved paddle enough to keep her hands away from her heated flesh.

She had been on her best behavior until Elbi

came up with an idea after the sun had set. She, and a few other women, had decided to sneak out to the nearby hot springs and wanted Cinder to come. She hadn't seen the hot springs since she had arrived, and the idea tempted her. She knew it was forbidden without permission, but the lure overtook any reason.

"What if someone finds out?" she asked in a whisper. Many of the other women were already asleep for the night.

"We take that risk. The worst thing that can happen is a punishment, and it will be worth it." Elbi giggled. "Who knows? Maybe we'll never be caught."

"I seriously doubt we won't get into trouble for this. The idea of doing this terrifies me."

Elbi shrugged. "If someone sees us, the punishment won't be so bad." She reached for Cinder's hand. "Come on, we won't get caught if we keep the noise down. Others in the harem are doing it, and you don't want to be left out."

Cinder almost refused, but the peer pressure was actually working on her. All reason screamed for her to remain in the palace, but she really wanted to see the hot springs and feel the night's fresh air against her skin. What was the worst thing that could happen? The springs were within the palace walls, so she'd still be safe. She wasn't putting her life at risk, and Elbi said the worst thing that could happen was a punishment... but what kind of punishment? Would Donte beat her if she were found? Would it be Mistress Krin, Mistress Tula, or Mistress Lana doing the beatings? She had yet to meet Mistress Lana and had only seen her in passing, but had heard stories that she was just as strict as the other two women when provoked. Cinder had hoped to never see that side of the woman, and yet here she was... provoking.

With a heavy heart, but also excitement sizzling through her core, Cinder nodded and stood with Elbi's hand intertwined with her own clammy palm. "I do want to go... I just hope I don't regret this."

"We'll be back before midnight," Elbi promised.

Hours were spent swimming and laughing. The sulphuric water, the warm air, and the starry sky made the risk worth whatever punishment lay in store. It was still hard for Cinder to believe at times that this was her new reality. No more struggle in the desert bouncing from commune to commune. The harem life was everything she imagined so far. Even more so.

Elbi swam up and spiritedly tried to dunk Cinder beneath the water. "I told you that you would have fun," she said.

Cinder smiled and nodded. "I am. I'm not used to... just relaxing and having a good time. I've also never had friends."

"You do now," Elbi said with a smile. "You fit in here perfectly. The other women adore you. I know it's hard to read them sometimes, but I know they do."

As Cinder watched the naked beauty float in the water before her, she decided to ask a question that had been plaguing her mind for awhile. "Elbi, have you ever met the prince?"

Elbi smiled, and her eyes twinkled in the moonlight. "Alone? Yes."

"What's he like? What did you do with him?"

"We aren't supposed to discuss our time with the prince. It's secret." Elbi glanced around and leaned in to whisper, "It's best you don't ask questions about him."

"Have you only met once?" A tinge of jealousy hit Cinder. She wondered why she hadn't met him yet.

Elbi looked at Cinder confused. "Privately? Just once but nothing happened other than discipline. I think he felt I wasn't ready for him yet, but I'm not sure because he never said. I'm waiting for the day he feels I've been trained enough for him." Elbi must have seen the envy on Cinder's face. "I'd been here a year before I was beckoned to his chambers alone. I thought it would never happen."

"What about the other women?" Cinder asked. "Do they go to the prince's chambers often?"

Elbi glanced around to make sure none of the other women were eavesdropping on their conversation. "We aren't allowed to speak of our time with the prince ever, so I don't know the answer to that and it is a rule that must not be broken."

Rolling her eyes, Cinder scoffed. "Isn't that what we're doing right now? Breaking the rules?"

Nodding, Elbi's expression became serious. "Yes, but while breaking some rules will only earn you a punishment, this rule is not one of those. Behind the door gossip is not allowed and being caught doing so would see you expelled from the harem." The air seemed thicker for a moment, as if her statement were a heavy weight hanging over them. But then Elbi grinned and splashed water at Cinder to lighten the mood. "But don't worry, you'll see for yourself soon enough. They'll know when you're ready."

Cinder watched Elbi swim off, taking in her voluptuous body as she floated above the surface of the water. She tried to allow Elbi's reassuring words to put her mind at ease, but she couldn't help but wonder why it took so long for the prince to summon her.

Soaking in the warm water, staring up into the sky, Cinder heard twigs breaking as someone approached. The sound of more heavy feet followed.

The shadowed figures on the bank signaled one thing—they had been caught. She had never seen the three mistresses lined up together before this moment, and their fearsome presence alone was frightening by itself... but nothing was more terrifying than Donte standing in front of them.

Donte's dark gaze darted to Cinder's, and she took a step back to the furthest bank of the spring due to the intensity on his firm features. She considered sinking into the water and never coming out. His glare alone was like a strike against her face. However, the severity of it quickly allayed as he scanned her nude body somewhat concealed by the water of the spring. Did he like what he saw, or could he see just how much Cinder trembled?

"Everyone exit the water immediately." He pointed at the ground in front of him and the mistresses. "I want complete silence." He scanned the distressed faces of each woman scampering out of the water, as he waited with his arms across his chest. "I see you all have dared to break the rules tonight. Apparently the Mistresses and I have been far too lenient with the harem."

Cinder exited the spring as quickly as everyone else and stood before him. Her eyes cast down to the puddle of water caused by her soaking wet body. As horrified and ashamed as she was to have been caught doing something she knew she shouldn't have, she couldn't help but feel exhilaration in the fact she got to breathe the same air as Donte again. It embarrassed her to admit how much she'd missed him in such a short time. Her guitar lessons didn't happen frequent enough in her opinion, and if acting out like an errant child kept him in her presence... then maybe she would have to be far less obedient.

When everyone stood before him, he paced back and forth. His expression did not change. "There are rules for safety. There are guidelines for submission. The harem has directives for order. These rules are to be respected. Have we not trained you all properly? Have we taught you nothing?"

"They need to be taught a lesson so they won't ever make this mistake again," Mistress Tula said in an even tone.

Donte nodded. "What time is it?"

"Nearly midnight," Mistress Krin answered.

"Very well. As punishment, I feel twelve lashes

is fair. Twelve lashes, twelve times," Donte said as small gasps escaped the lips of the women standing at attention.

Cinder swallowed against the dryness in her throat, confused by her growing desire with each of Donte's firm words. His voice, his dominance, his stare. She stood before Donte completely nude and at his mercy. The need for his discipline overwhelmed her, though twelve lashes twelve times sounded far harsher than she felt she could handle. Cinder looked up from the ground and made eye contact with him. His eyes darkened before he averted them from hers. He remained still for a moment, silent, as he scanned the beautiful bodies before him.

"You will all be punished for your disobedience." Cinder looked down at the ground again. "Follow Mistress Krin, Mistress Tula and Mistress Lana to the main room. They'll deliver your punishment... severely."

Cinder couldn't help but feel disappointment as well as extreme fear. She didn't want discipline by the hand of one of the mistresses. She wanted Donte. She would prefer a far worst beating from Donte if it meant the punishment came from him rather than one of the three sisters.

"Except for Cinder," he quickly added. "Since I have yet to issue a true punishment to you, I will handle your correction myself." Cinder didn't have to look up to know he was watching her. She could feel the intensity of his scrutiny.

She remained in the blackness of her own shame as the other women followed the mistresses back to the palace. She saw pity in Elbi's eyes as her friend mouthed the words, "Stay strong."

Donte placed his hand on her lower back, reminding her of when they first met, and led her to the palace as well.

"We will go to my quarters to deal with your behavior alone."

Mortification limited her to answer with nothing more than, "Yes, sir."

"You have been naughty, Cinder. You give me no choice but to punish you. You understand that, correct?" he asked as his eyes traveled to her exposed breasts, only inches from his body.

"I understand." Her voice cracked as they headed up the steps to the palace.

As soon as she arrived, he gestured for her to close the door, but he didn't turn to face her. She stopped a few feet away after doing as she was bid. Hesitation tangled at her feet before she finally knelt before him.

"Good girl." He finally turned to face her, but his expression was somber, verging on grim. "I'm pleased to see fear in your eyes."

"My apologies, sir. It will not happen again." Cinder ducked her head repentantly and stared at her hands, folded as they were in her lap.

"I will see that it does not."

"Yes, sir."

The silence that hung after her words was painful, and she fought the urge to lift her head and look upon his face. It was only when he closed the distance between them and touched her chin with his fingers that she was permitted to look.

She tried to look down at the ground so she wouldn't have to see the disapproval in his eyes, but he held her chin in place, glaring into hers.

"You will be punished for your behavior tonight harsher than you have ever been before. Disobedience is not to be tolerated. Is that understood?"

He didn't so much as smile. His fingers released her chin and, without the support, her head simply dropped forward again. Her breath caught in her chest and everything went dim around her. Cinder felt terribly faint and her fingers tightened in her sweaty palms, desperate to clutch something, anything at all, for support.

"Of course, sir. I-I understand." The words barely squeaked out, breathless and aching. She looked up into his stern face, and the tears that had built in her eyes finally dared to stream forth. "I'm sorry. I shouldn't have—"

"Go kneel in the corner."

The command shook her nerves, and Cinder uttered a small moan of fear, mixed with aroused anticipation.

"Now."

She shuddered, rushing to the corner as he demanded. She could smell the dust mingling with her tears. She could feel her breath bounce off the wall against her face and hear the quivering of it all the more keenly.

It felt like an eternity before his hand came to rest on the back of her head. He stroked his fingers through her hair and whispered in her ear, "You are a good girl, Cinder. I will be much easier on you than I had intended because of your obvious submission. You will not receive the same punishment as the rest of the harem. But from this moment on, I expect you to obey the rules of the harem for there will be no more exceptions or special treatment."

Donte took hold of her hair and yanked her to standing. The sting to her scalp had her yelping in surprise more than distress. He then released his grip of her hair and gently placed the tresses over her shoulder. His fingertips caressed her spine, moving lower down until he made small circles on the cheeks of her ass—each caress languid and easy. He had a masterful touch, demanding compliance before the first sting of correction. Cinder stared at the marble floor, readying herself for the punishment in store.

She took a deep breath and closed her eyes as the first slap made contact with her bottom. A fire broke out over her flesh as his hand showered a spanking very different than the first one. This one hurt. This one hurt in the most shocking of ways. All control she thought she possessed escaped her as she begged for mercy. Her cries, mixed with spank after spank, rang off the walls. His heavy breath merged with her sobs as his hand landed over and over against the inferno of her behind.

"Please!" she called out. "Donte, please. It hurts."

"Yes, Cinder. A punishment does."

Spank after spank flooded upon her, each one building in intensity. The power of his hand rivaled any wooden paddle or leather strap.

Just as she was sure her body had reached its maximum capacity to accept his discipline, the thunderous waves of punishment ceased. She stared at the floor, watching her own tears cascade down into a puddle.

But after the briefest of moments, the punishment resumed and she understood. This was meant to break her. She could tell.

She could feel.

He swatted her naked ass as she remained in the corner. The searing spanks shocked her, weakening her legs, threatening to buckle her knees. Still, he continued to spank as her face remained inches from the wall.

"This time, I will only use my hand against your flesh. But if you dare sneak out at night again, you will feel the sting of leather." He spanked with each syllable of his spoken words.

She cried. Not because of the hurt, but because she desperately wanted to feel his warmth beneath her by being placed over his knee. Standing alone in the corner was far worse than any form of correction she could have imagined.

The spanking seemed endless, swat after swat, each one growing harder than the one before. "Please... please, sir!" The sniveling wasn't comely and she knew it. He reminded her of it by withdrawing his hand and walking away. She could hear him move across the room, could imagine him turning his back to her. She started to cry even harder, and the weight of his silence only made it worse.

He returned and stood behind her. His body was so close that she could almost feel his heat. Cinder gasped when he grabbed her butt and spread her cheeks. He placed a moist finger at her anus and pressed firmly but without entering. "If I wanted to claim your ass right now, could I?" He pressed his finger past her tight entrance.

Cinder tensed and bit her lip to not cry out.

He thrust his finger deeper. "You understand that I can punish your asshole for your actions tonight as well?"

Cinder nodded, because finding words was impossible in her heated state.

Donte pumped his finger in and out a few more times and then withdrew it completely, replacing it with the cool glass of a butt plug. He inserted it without pause. The stretch to her anus caused her to clench, which only elevated the biting sting.

"You are dismissed, Cinder. The next time you try to sneak out at night, I won't be so merciful. Remember that. Return to the harem." His dismissive command stabbed at her heart.

She wasn't sure how she was going to walk out of the room, but she managed to. Just barely. She staggered up and went for the door at a near run, all the while pawing at the loose wisps of her hair and the tears that streaked her face. She didn't look to see him—but she didn't want to. It would have hurt entirely too much. His lack of comfort, or a soothing embrace, was by far the worst punishment she had yet received.

9

It wasn't the sunlight peeking through the window, or the stirrings of the women of the harem that woke Cinder from her slumber. It was the soft shaking of her shoulder. It was Donte hovering over her. She had been punished by him rather than the mistresses, and now rewarded by his morning presence.

"Good morning, Cinder." Donte spoke her name with a soft intimacy.

"Good morning." She moved her body just enough so she could look into his eyes.

"I would like you to join me for breakfast this morning," Donte said.

Glancing around, she could see the other women still fast asleep. Their punishments had been harsh and each woman was sobbing in pain as she had reentered the room last night. It took them a long time to settle down and finally fall asleep.

She nodded, feeling special. "All right."

A loud knock at the door had both of them jumping up in surprise. Donte directed, "Stay where you are." He walked to the door as the rest of the harem still slept soundly. It didn't appear as if the knock had disturbed their slumber.

He opened the door, but stood in the doorway blocking Cinder's view of who stood on the other side. The loud voice from the hallway surprised her in its urgency. "We just got word from the scout. It's as we feared."

"How many?" Donte asked. His spine stiffened against the doorframe.

"Enough. More than we could handle."

"Start our plan in action."

"Sir, we did not take into account the sheer numbers."

Cinder's heart skipped. She pulled the satin sheet she slept with up to shield her nudity. Something scared her about the concern in both the men's voices.

Donte nodded. "I understand that. But for now, move forward with the plan, and we'll address the rest later." He closed the door and made his way back to where she slept. "I'm sorry you had to hear that."

"Is it Jaden?" Cinder asked, not considering that her question could be crossing a line.

Donte's eyebrow rose. "I am surprised your mind went straight to Jaden."

"Is it?"

Donte paused, studied her for a moment, and then nodded. "Yes."

"Are they coming to attack us?" Fear paralyzed her.

Donte patted her arm reassuringly. "No need to worry."

Cinder pulled away, not remembering her harem rules of submission. "Please don't coddle me like a child. Is Jaden and its army coming here?"

He stood as a storm washed over his eyes. "It's not your concern."

"But I can help. I was there. I might have information that can help you prepare."

Donte ran his hand through his tousled hair. "It is time you wake the harem." He walked to the door and looked over his shoulder. "I have matters I need to attend to. I am sure you can manage with your own breakfast." The door slammed behind him as fear roiled in her stomach.

CINDER SENSED his presence the moment he walked in. Donte—the man she hadn't been able to get out of her mind since she arrived at the harem—was staring at her as she did her morning exercise with Maysa. Up and down the courtyard stairs had become their usual routine. Maysa had lightheartedly informed Cinder that a firm butt was a necessity. Cinder didn't mind the climbing of stairs unless a larger than normal plug was planted firmly in her bottom. Regardless, she and Maysa never faltered from their habitual workout.

She picked up her pace a little, her emotions getting the best of her. There was something about him that made her heart beat faster, her core seemed to heat up, and she couldn't control her need to stare. She knew she was here for the prince, but after last night, Cinder wanted to give her body fully to Donte. As she watched him stride across the courtyard to where Mistress Krin stood, she nearly stumbled on her next step.

"Careful there," Maysa warned. "Why are you going so fast? The plug in my behind is demanding I take this a bit slower."

Cinder watched the pained expression on her friend's face and giggled. She slowed her climb with a wink.

She couldn't help but stare at Donte as he discussed something that seemed of importance with Mistress Krin. Cinder's gaze dropped to the bulge in his pants. She wished she had been able to please him after she had been punished. Cinder had researched what women do to please a man before she had set out on her journey to the palace. Though pure in body, she had trained her mind in what would be expected once she arrived. She understood the workings of a man in both body and thought. She could almost taste the saltiness of his sex at the wicked thought. The image of his cock, inches from her face, would become her new fantasy.

What was wrong with her?

Why had this obsession become so all consuming and powerful?

She was here to be part of the prince's harem. Not to be with Donte.

Swiping at her loose hair, her pulse sped as she glanced his way. Donte's steely eyes made contact with hers. He stood with his arms across his chest as he studied the way she marched up the steps. Never taking his eyes off her, he leaned and whispered something to Mistress Krin. He appeared... angry. Had she done something wrong?

He took large strides her way and stood at the bottom of the stairs. "Cinder, I would like a word with you."

She stopped and made her way to where he

stood, noticing that Maysa continued her climb, no doubt wanting to avoid Donte's wrath.

"Follow me." He turned and headed to the palace. Cinder hesitated for a moment, but quickly followed step.

They entered a part of the palace she had never been in. Donte opened a large wooden door and motioned for her to precede him. A quick scan of the room informed her they were not alone. Hovering by a large table were two uniformed men who had swords hanging from their sides. They appeared different than the guards she had seen around the palace. They scanned her body, making Cinder grateful she wasn't nude though their razor-sharp glares made her feel as if they were cutting away the delicate silk of her wrap. Fear crowded in. She stopped walking and waited until Donte stood beside her.

His hand pressed firmly against her lower back, not giving her the reassuring feeling it once did. Something was wrong.

"We have some questions we need to ask you," Donte said evenly as he led her to a chair. "We want to know why you came to the Palace of Lazar," he continued.

She took a seat, desperately wanting to escape the men's stares. "I told you. I wanted something different from what most communes offered."

"Why did you leave the commune of Briar?" one of the uniformed men asked. Even though it was a question, it sounded as if it were an order.

Her heart stopped. She didn't want to talk about her past. She looked down at the ground. "It was overcrowded."

"So your family left?" the man continued.

Cinder shook her head. Tears welled in the backs of her eyes, but she willed herself to keep them at bay.

"You left alone?" the man pressed.

She nodded.

"So, you are saying that as a young woman, you left your birth commune all alone because you felt it was too crowded?"

Cinder hated the tone of this man's voice.

She nodded again, refusing to look at anyone.

The man walked over and slammed his hand on the table, causing Cinder to jump in her seat. "Look at me when I speak to you!"

Donte closed in and pushed the man back. "Enough." His order was sharp, direct and unyielding. "Address the lady with respect."

The uniformed man glared at Cinder, but walked to the other side of the table.

His suspicious eyes examined her closely as he spoke. "Briar is further than most men can journey. Tell me how a young girl, all alone, trekked her way through the desert and landed here."

Cinder looked at Donte who nodded slightly, giving her the strength to answer. "I didn't have a choice." She took a breath, now feeling like a weight rested on her chest. "Briar reached capacity and began to evict the sick, weak, and old. I wasn't any of those, but my grandmother was. I couldn't allow an old woman to be cast into the desert alone. How would she survive? What would she do?" Cinder swiped at a fleeing tear. "So I gave her my space in the commune. My chances of surviving the desert were greater than hers. I at least had a chance."

"So where did you go?" the man pressed.

Cinder looked down at the ground but continued. "I traveled the desert for two days when I reached the commune of Luge. I stayed there for a few days and then journeyed to the commune of Salen." Cinder looked up and met his stare. "I've been to thirteen communes, with one goal. My final destination was the Palace of Lazar."

"What about Jaden? How long were you in Jaden?" He continued with the interrogation.

She looked at Donte who studied her every move. She remained silent.

"Answer the question," Donte encouraged.

"Why are you asking me these questions?"

The man slammed his hand on the table again. "Answer the question!"

Donte glared at the man. "I won't warn you again. You will not speak to her in any way but with respect!"

The man huffed, but acquiesced by sitting down.

She studied the interrogating man and realized what was happening. "You think I'm a spy for Jaden. They're getting ready to attack, and you think they sent me. Don't you?"

She looked up at Donte whose stare never wavered.

"You think I was sent here to help them take over. You don't believe my story. Do you?"

Her gaze was turned to the man when he spoke, venom dripping with each word. "I don't think a young woman could possibly travel the distance you claim. I also don't think it's possible that you could have survived the journey from even Jaden, let alone Briar, without help."

Cinder looked back at Donte. "What about you? Do you think Jaden sent me?" Panic almost paralyzed her. What would they do if they thought she was a spy? Would they kill her? Cast her out into the desert? What would happen if they didn't believe her story?

"How long were you in Jaden?" Donte asked.

"A week... a little over a week. I was there long enough to see that they were building their army. But I wasn't part of it. I swear!" Fear caused her voice to crack.

"Tell us what you know about Jaden," Donte ordered softly.

Cinder watched each man as they studied every move and every word she released. She could tell they thought she knew more than she was letting on. She knew this was her only chance to convince them her actions were true.

"Every man and woman of strength was being turned in to soldiers. Jaden was one of the few communes actively requesting new residents. The word spread fast in the other communes. Jaden became the destination of many pilgrimages. When I arrived, I soon saw that Jaden was no different than any other community. Overpopulation, disease, hate, crime—just like the rest of them. But what Jaden had that the others didn't, was structure. The militant environment frightened me. Power-hungry soldiers stood on every corner." She paused to take a deep breath. "Tents were being set up outside the city boundaries to house even more soldiers. Blacksmiths were brought in to create more weapons. I've never seen anything like it. Jaden was by far the largest commune I had seen."

"Did you ever see a water source?" Donte asked.

"What do you mean?"

"Did you see a lake? A river? A large well of some sort? Where did the residents get their water?"

"There was a lake in the middle," she said. "There were large pumps coming from the lake, so I guess they got it from there."

Donte began to pace the room. "What type of weapons? What were the blacksmiths making?"

Cinder pointed to the sword on the uniformed man's leg. "Swords like that one. It seemed that there were more weapons than food."

Donte's eyebrow rose. "Food? Was food scarce?"

Cinder nodded. "Just like every other commune."

The uniformed man added, "And yet they were taking in more residents..."

"What about horses? Did they have horses?" Donte asked, worry washed over his face.

Cinder shook her head confused. "Horses? I told you that food was scarce."

"Were they riding horses?" he asked.

Cinder didn't know what he was talking about. Why would they ride on their food source?

"Cinder, did you see any of the soldiers riding horses?"

Cinder shook her head. "I didn't see any

animals, but then the first time I've seen any animals is when I got here." The Palace of Lazar had livestock grazing, peacocks roaming the grounds, sheep in the distance. For the first time, Cinder had seen animals not just used for slaughter.

Donte nodded. "That is enough for now." He looked at the men. "Gentlemen, I believe Cinder has been asked enough questions."

He reached for her hand and assisted her out of the chair. He placed his palm on her lower back and escorted her out of the room. She could feel the glares of the men, but with Donte's touch, she no longer had any fear.

10

Cinder walked down the hallway and mentally prepared herself for what would come next. Did they think she was a spy? Was Donte going to ask her to leave the harem?

Donte's tall frame towered over her. If she had any doubt of his strength, the way he conducted himself with the other men proved he was a man not to mess with.

His gaze found hers, his eyes as blue as the water that cascaded out of the fountains blanketing the palace and so piercing at the same time.

She caught her breath, not being able to control the yearning that sliced through her at his nearness. He led them toward his private quarters.

"I have some further issues to discuss with you," he said as he led her past the entrance.

"Do you believe that Jaden sent me?" she asked, her voice not much more than a whisper.

"I believe you came here on your own free will."

Cinder swallowed hard. He didn't fully answer her question.

Donte reached up to caress the smooth line of her jaw. "I believe you are the strongest woman I have ever met. I believe you managed to do things and travel distances that no man could do. You sacrificed yourself for the sake of a loved one. I have not met anyone who would do that."

Her eyes glittered with tears, the words stinging her soul.

"I have never admired a woman before," he said, his finger moving to tease her lower lip, torturing her with such a gentle touch. He sighed and stepped backward, his hand dropping away.

It was a struggle not to reach for him, to not fall into his embrace, to not feel his intimate touch. She remembered the way his hand felt against her skin, how the discipline of last night had her moaning for more. The hunger for his cock almost took her breath away. It must have been all the training, but she had never felt so sexual and passionate before. She'd never once thought of a man's member before arriving at the Palace of Lazar. All this time being trained as a harem girl had left her thirstier than any day in the desert.

She desperately wanted her thirst quenched by his seed.

She wanted to give herself to him. She wanted it even more than serving the prince of the palace. But she was also afraid. Her virginity belonged to the prince as it was part of being in the harem.

Donte's voice brought her back to the present. "We are going to have to evacuate the harem," he said, turning away and walking toward a window to stare out.

"What? Why?" Her heart stopped. She wondered if she'd faint right there. She knew what his answer would be.

Resting an arm on the windowsill, with his back facing her, he answered, "Jaden is planning their attack on the palace. We aren't prepared, and although we plan to fight, the battle will not be in our favor." He turned to face her. "We're going to split up the harem and have you all go to different communes. We have neighboring allies who will assist us in our time of need. But in the meantime, we have to make sure the women cannot be taken hostage. Capturing the harem would be quite the prize and offer bragging rights. No matter what, even with the fall of Lazar, we'll not give them the harem."

Cinder shook her head, not knowing what to

say, but positive she didn't like what she was hearing.

Donte continued, "I'm going to ask you to lead one of the groups. You clearly understand the land and the ruthless nature of the desert. You're a fighter, and I have no doubt you can lead your group to safety."

Cinder's ears rang, her breath ragged. She shook her head again, but remained silent.

"We feel breaking the harem in three groups will be the best. We need all the guards to stay and fight, so we have no choice but to send the women alone. I will put Mistress Krin and Mistress Lana in charge of the largest group with the weaker of the women, and Mistress Tula in charge of the other. But the remaining one will be led by you."

Words escaped her. She wanted to scream no, but her voice was lost in her ocean of fear.

"It will be expected that you lead your group, and wait for us to retrieve you."

Cinder finally found the words. "I want to stay with you," she whispered hoarsely. "Let us stay and fight. At least let *me* stay and fight."

Donte shook his head. "You would not be a help, but a hindrance. I cannot have my men worried about the safety of the harem, when they need to be worrying about their own lives."

The words stung even though they were true.

Donte crossed the room in three long strides to where she stood. "I need you, Cinder. I need your strength to keep you and the other women safe. I need you to do this for me."

Cinder shook her head vehemently. "No. I can't."

"I am not asking. I am commanding."

"No! No! No!"

She shook her head, hysteria washing over her. They were going to die. Donte, the prince, the guards, even the harem. They were all going to die.

"No!" she screamed. Breathing became harder, her heart threatened to rip out of her chest.

Donte grabbed her by the shoulders and shook. "Cinder, look at me. Control yourself. I have no doubt you can do this. I *need* you to be able to do this."

His mouth descended. His kiss conquered her lips as she so desperately hoped he would conquer Jaden.

Passion erupted, a fervor stronger than any power known to man. His kiss dominated every sense in her body. It demanded every emotion, every feeling. Everything in her became his with one demanding kiss. She couldn't breathe, couldn't reason, couldn't put up any resistance as his strong arms swooped her up and carried her over to his bed. And fear of the future erased within his arms.

Without saying a word, he removed her silk in one fluid motion. She stood at the edge completely nude. It wasn't the first time she stood naked before him, but this time was different. Her body sizzled beneath his hungry stare. Lust melted her core. Her pussy throbbed in anticipation.

"Lay down." His command was husky.

Cinder parted her lips with bated breath.

The nearby candlelight fired his ebony hair, his face glowed in the warm light. His hard edges softened as he pressed the palm of her hand against his chest. She could feel his heart beat against her touch. He never released her of his stare as the rhythm of his life pounded against her hand. One beat at a time, the bond between the two shaped.

He kissed her again, dominating her mouth with slow thoroughness. His lips pressed firmly to hers as his tongue plunged deep within her mouth. Pulling away, he placed soft kisses down her neck, along her shoulder, slowly lowering until his tongue teased her erect nipple.

Her body shuddered in response to the touch. A gasp escaped her lips as his mouth sucked her nipple completely. Lost in erotic touch, Cinder's mind eddied beneath her closed eyes. He moved to the other hardened nipple, edging her closer and closer to a cliff of uninhibited fervor.

With a stream of kisses down her stomach, Donte placed his body between her spread legs. Stroking her moistened folds, he skillfully plunged his finger into her pussy. Cinder tensed at the surprise penetration, but relaxed as he massaged his way in. He began a seductive dance with his finger, in and out of her wet entrance. Looking into her eyes, he lowered his mouth to her clit and circled his tongue along the bud. Gentle licks with rougher thrusts of his finger pulled a moan from the depths of Cinder's core.

"Wait here," he commanded as he got off the bed.

When Cinder turned to see why he had stopped, she found him undressing. Once naked, Donte resumed his position.

"Did you like that?" he asked huskily.

A moan was her only answer.

Returning his finger to her pussy, he soon added a second one and pressed even deeper. "Do you like your pussy being spread wide?"

She arched her back and moaned even louder.

Keeping his fingers planted in her pussy, Donte leaned forward and took her breast into his mouth. He sucked and nibbled as Cinder's pleasure grew. He pulled away from her pebbled nipple just enough to ask, "Do you want more?"

Nodding, her whimper speaking of her desire,

she was rewarded by Donte thrusting his fingers in and out of her pussy over and over again. He wasn't being gentle, but he also wasn't being overly aggressive or rough.

"I want to fuck you, Cinder," he growled as he took her other breast into his mouth with a little more force than the last time. "I want to fuck you and make you mine."

"Yes, sir. Please," she begged.

In one fluid motion, he pulled his fingers out of her wet pussy and placed his cock at the entrance, applying pressure but not breaking past. He paused and looked into her eyes. "Are you truly a virgin, Cinder?"

She nodded, suddenly scared that he would stop. She should save herself for the prince, but she didn't care. Donte is whom she wanted to belong to.

His. Forever his.

He had become her fairytale.

He had become her truth.

"Will you allow me to claim you as mine? May I take your virginity?"

She nodded again and smiled. "Yes, sir. Please."

"You traveled all this way to service the prince. Wouldn't you rather give yourself to royalty? To a prince who could give you all kinds of riches?"

"I know being part of the harem means

servicing the prince, but I no longer care. I want you. I can't help it. It's a need stronger than I can explain."

Donte placed his lips gently to hers. A slight buzz rang in her ears, and all she could do was open her lips slightly, allowing him access with his tongue. Donte wasted no time and delved his tongue in, deepening the conquest of her mouth. He applied a little more pressure with his cock at her pussy as he continued to kiss.

After what felt like an everlasting embrace, he pulled away and whispered, "This will hurt for a moment. Cry out against my mouth."

With that command, his lips once again crushing hers, Donte pressed his cock all the way into her virginal pussy in one quick motion. There was a startling pop, followed by a biting pain. Cinder did as he ordered and cried out against his kiss, allowing him to swallow up her pain. He remained still once he was fully planted inside her.

"Shhh... relax. The pain will subside in a few moments," he soothed.

Yes, there was some pain, but the hunger for more overruled any other sensation. Cinder was the one to begin moving her hips in hopes of more. Donte didn't need any further coaxing. He began to thrust his cock in and out of her welcoming pussy with a rhythm that almost hypnotized her. He lowered his finger to her clit and applied pressure as he circled around her nub. Her juices of arousal coated his dick, making each thrust of his cock wetter than the last.

He nibbled on her neck and whispered, "Allow the sensations. Feel the pain, feel the pleasure, feel me as I claim what is, and always will be, mine. This virgin pussy is now mine. There is no turning back."

Over and over his cock pumped into her. The steady passion reminded her of a drum, beating her way to orgasm. She had imagined what this day would be like, but hadn't even come close to the pure ecstasy that coursed through her core. Pump after pump of his hard cock brought her closer and closer to a peak she knew she wanted to reach. And once she reached it... she jumped off into an explosion of pleasure that shook her body. A scream escaped her lips as it was met with a guttural moan from Donte as he too leapt off that peak.

As his seed spilled inside her body, she lay limp beneath his weight. Chills of pleasure danced along her skin, followed by the soft kisses of Donte. She savored what had happened, feeling alive, free, and for a brief moment... safe.

She knew that was all about to change.

Her fairytale was about to morph to a war.

A deadly and dangerous war.

But for this very moment... she had found her Prince Charming. Her happily ever after.

Regardless for how long... her story had ended how she had always pictured it.

For now...

11

Donte stood before Cinder and spoke in a low voice. "These women have been instructed to follow your orders." Cinder looked over at the five frightened women behind her. "You are to head west for a couple of days. You'll run into a commune that has been mostly abandoned." He reached for her chin and tilted it up so she was staring directly into his eyes. "Wait there for me. I'll come and get you all."

"Can Elbi come with me?" Maysa was one of the five women standing behind her, but Elbi had been assigned to another group.

Donte shook his head. "The groups have been decided." When Cinder looked down at the ground in defeat, Donte tilted her chin back up. "Elbi will be fine. I assure you. There's been a bounty placed on all of your heads. We need to do whatever we can to protect you."

Tears clouded Cinder's vision. "What about you?" She should probably worry about the prince as well and where he would go, but had no doubt his best men would protect him with their lives. But what about Donte? Who would protect him?

"I stay and fight. Once our allies arrive, we plan on stopping the enemy before they even reach the palace. We have horses and will meet them in the desert. They'll be hot and exhausted from the journey. We will not."

"Then let us stay."

"We've been over this, Cinder. This is a precaution. It's our job to make sure that Jaden cannot get their hands on you." He smiled softly and whispered, "I'll find you and bring you back. Wait for me."

He took a couple of steps back and declared in a loud voice. "I know you are all frightened, but Cinder knows the desert well. Listen to her, obey her, and all will be fine." Cinder glanced at Maysa who nodded and gave a smile of support.

"WE'RE NOT THAT FAR," Cinder said, gesturing off into the distance.

Maysa stared in frustration, her hands on her hips. She looked to where Cinder was pointing, but there wasn't anything in the distance to see. Maysa looked from the horizon to her and back again.

"We're not that far from what?" she asked.

"From the commune," Cinder answered. "We've been traveling for two days now. I can tell we're getting closer."

Maysa dug a flask from her satchel. "The girls are tired. They're worried you're getting us lost."

"I'm fine," Cinder said when Maysa extended the flask to her. She shook her head firmly and only looked at the horizon.

The idea of cool, crisp, refreshing water sounded like a delightful change from the dry heat they had been experiencing for the past days, but they needed to conserve all the water they had. Cinder didn't know when they would find resources next. She knew there was water out there somewhere, but she didn't know how far away it was. Her only hope was that the commune would have some.

Maysa held the flask out to her and insisted. "No, you need to drink. I can tell you're trying to save all the water and food for everyone else, but we need you healthy."

"I'm *fine*," she said firmly as she pushed Maysa's hand away. She felt guilty for snapping, but her patience had worn out. She'd been carrying the bags of the other women when they complained they couldn't go on. The extra weight and her self-imposed rations had taken their toll.

Taking the bags hadn't helped as much as she hoped. The women were weakening with every step toward nowhere. Their progress slowed as she had to keep stopping to allow them to rest. She hated to show signs of weakness, especially in front of Maysa, but she needed the rest just as much as they did.

"We'll rest here for a bit. Take a small drink of water, but remember it needs to last," Cinder called out to the women. She pulled a ragged piece of cloth from her satchel and sat next to Maysa on the sand. Carefully, she pushed back her hair, which nearly blended in with the color of the sand, and wrapped the cloth around her head.

Maysa did the same with another piece of cloth from her satchel, covering her crop of dark hair. The cloth was the same tan as her skin. Her dark eyes were sunken with exhaustion, enough to make Cinder worry about her friend. She feared the intense heat would claim one of them soon if they didn't find the commune.

"How long can we rest?" Maysa asked, taking another sip of her water.

Cinder looked at the other women sitting

nearby. "Until I feel the girls can get back on their feet," she answered, brushing sweat from her forehead.

Maysa reached over and patted Cinder's leg. "Donte would be really proud of you."

Cinder sat in silence, but smiled.

"You have feelings for him, don't you?"

Cinder looked down at the sand and nodded.

"You'll see him again. I'm sure of it."

The tears threatened to fall. "I hope so."

Cinder refused to show any sign of weakness. Immediately, she leapt to her feet, pausing to clear the darkness from her eyes from rising too quickly. She regained her vision and declared, "Let's get moving. The time we waste sitting here, is time we could spend finding the commune."

With that, they started off.

Two and a half days in the desert. Walking over dune after dune with five women tested everything she had. They needed her strength. They relied on her encouragement and prodding. They required her leadership to help them through this awful expedition. Cinder doubted her own resolve many times, but knew other's lives were in her hands. Step after step, she powered through.

"Is that it?" Maysa asked, breathing heavily as the sun was about to set.

Cinder nodded as she looked at her dear

friend. Poor Maysa looked haggard. Matted hair, chapped lips, and burned skin claimed all of the beautiful harem women standing under the relentless sun.

Cinder spoke loud enough for everyone to hear. "We're almost there. We'll go into the commune and find shelter for the night."

When they finally spotted the skyline of a small commune ahead, they were united in their tears of joy. They had reached their destination! They had survived. They made it.

As they entered the town, Cinder couldn't help but wonder how long they would have to stay. When would Donte return? She wasn't naïve. She knew there was a real possibility of him not returning at all. Jaden had the manpower and the weapons to wipe out Lazar completely. She could lose Donte to the sword of a Jaden warrior.

Cinder scanned the village as they cautiously walked down the street. It appeared abandoned. No people, no life, no civilization. She tried to take stock of where their water source may have been. It might have dried up, which would explain why the commune had been abandoned. Finding food would be futile, and Cinder worried how long the women's rations would last. She spotted a building that appeared still in good shape and decided it would be their home for the night—if not longer.

Pure exhaustion took over as the women entered the building and settled in for the night. The trip through the desert was by far the hardest thing most of them had ever done. Cinder had done worse, but after reaching Lazar, she'd thought her desert nomad days were over.

Maysa came and sat down next to her on the floor. "Now what?"

Cinder shrugged. "We wait."

"How long do you think it will take until they come to get us?"

Cinder shrugged again. "I don't know. We have three or four more days of food and water. If they don't come by then, we'll have to find it ourselves." She paused a moment to ponder. "I think tomorrow we'll go and explore the city and see if we can find anything."

"It doesn't look like anything was left behind," Maysa said.

"No, it doesn't." Cinder watched as Maysa took off her shoes, the soles of her feet a mass of pus-filled blisters, bruising and swelling. She was pretty sure her feet, as well as the rest of the women's feet, all looked the same.

"You did well, Cinder. I'm happy you were our leader and—"

Cinder cut Maysa off by raising her hand and

motioning for silence. She thought she heard something. Footsteps?

"Get your shoes on," she whispered. "Everyone, get your stuff and get ready to run on my word." Cinder paused, listening for the sound again. The women scurried to collect their items and stood with terror on their faces.

Silence.

She listened hard, only hearing her breath and the heavy breathing of the women.

Silence.

And then the words...

"Stay right where you are." A man walked into the room with an axe in his hand.

Cinder turned to Maysa. "Run! Run now and don't look back. Take them and run! I'll hold him off."

Maysa hesitated.

"Go! Everyone run!" Cinder screamed.

The man charged, but Cinder met his attack head on. She plowed into his body with all her weight, knocking them both to the ground. She could see that the women had escaped from the corner of her eye which was all she cared about. These women were hers to protect. It was her responsibility.

She would do whatever it took to protect them. She was their leader.

Before she could register relief, the man's fist hit her face with a storming force. Bolts of light blurred her vision from the power of the blow. Blood seeped from her nose as her attacker punched her again and again like a ravaging beast. The evil in his eyes shone in the dim light of the abandoned building. The rot of his teeth and the stench of his breath only enhanced the nightmare Cinder couldn't wake from. This monster was decaying with the rest of the world, but it was clear his soul and any human decency had already disappeared.

Seeing her blood splattered on the ground, she struggled to her feet, but he was suddenly on top of her, restraining her on the sand-covered floor, his filthy clad thighs prying her legs apart. She tried not to focus on the crazed face looming over her. His hungry eyes laced with evil made it clear he wanted more than just murder and mayhem.

He would rape her. He would rape her and then he would kill her. Cinder was sure she wasn't his first victim and most certainly wouldn't be his last. There were thousands like this man. The world had created them. A new breed. A sick and twisted version of what man once was.

His mouth came down toward her face, dried spit and crusted sand at the corners. She blocked the forced vile touch with both hands, flaying his skin with her nails as she attempted to claw out his eyes. Cinder fought the urge to let out a scream, she feared Maysa or the others would come back to try to save her. She wouldn't allow that. She wouldn't allow them all to die. She had no choice but to save herself. Even if she died, this man wouldn't walk away unscathed.

She would kill him if she could.

She would die fighting and bring this man with her to the depths of hell.

He hissed between his missing teeth, beads of foul sweat dripped off the tip of his filthy nose. Sweat oozed from every pore of his body. Clearly fatigue had set in. Cinder could feel his strength weakening with every defensive move she made. His depraved desires clouded his mind. Hope washed over her. She could still fight him off. She just needed to outlast his vigor. Resilience and wits could switch this situation around. She wouldn't stop fighting until he killed her.

"You are nothing but a whore! You know you want it just as bad as me. You're one of the harem girls. We've heard all about the harem girls. You want it! Stop fighting!"

Breathing hard, his desert-worn body wheezed with every struggle. He had her detained on the hot, sandy floor, but Cinder knew she had a chance to break free as his sexual need overpowered everything else. Nutrition, rest, and exercise at the palace had made her strong. She thrashed her body more, refusing to look at his lust-filled face only inches from her own. As the battle continued, she suddenly doubted that strength alone would fight him off. Cinder feared he would eventually win. She needed something—

His axe. She needed to reach his axe.

She had sent it flying across the room when she'd met his attack head on. If only she could stretch out her arm just a little further, the weapon would be within reach. She needed to struggle more. Just a little bit more.

"Stop fighting! I'll kill you if I have to!" Spittle splattered Cinder's face. Nausea roiled through her.

His soiled hands grabbed her breasts. Lust distracted him, slowly letting his guard down. "You know you want this. This is what you women are trained for. I heard all about the harem," he murmured, despicable vile warred with lust in his voice. "It's been so long. So long. So long!"

Cinder opened her mouth to scream, but stifled her voice. Her only chance of getting out of this alive was to outsmart him. Catch him off guard.

Reach for the axe.

"I used to be a ladies' man," he continued, moving a hand to unbutton his pants. "I promise you, I'll make you feel good. Real good. I know you're experienced, but I can teach you a thing or two."

She managed to fake a smile and nod.

"Just stop fighting me," he spat. "Spread your legs. You want me, don't you?"

"Yes," she whispered, the word almost burning her tongue. "You're right. I'm a harem girl. I know *exactly* what to do."

His severe stare searched her face. "You're not going to fight, right? You're going to stay right here where you belong and let me fuck that tight pussy of yours?"

She managed another weak nod and an even bigger smile.

He returned the smile, a sneer that revealed gaps where teeth once were. His thighs relaxed, loosening their hold on her lower body.

Cinder forced herself to be patient. She had to wait for just the right opportunity to strike. She knew she would have only one chance. Cinder would die before she'd let the monster take her.

The man slowly shifted so he could lower his pants.

Axe. There was the axe.

She smiled one last time before she shoved him away, rolled toward the axe, and swung. It happened so quick, Cinder didn't have time to think. She let out an animalistic growl as she struck the axe into his chest.

Blood sputtered from his mouth as he glanced down at his body in horror. She'd just missed his heart. Blood poured from the wound. His blood-shot eyes flashed with rage as he knocked the axe out of her hand, sending it flying across the room once again.

Turning her head, she saw the axe lying across the room. Wincing, she managed to fight her way into a standing position, head still spinning from the battering blows to her face. She drew in a deep breath, stumbling as she made her way across the room.

Cinder stood inches from the axe when her attacker shot up from the floor, evidently thinking the same as her. Not giving him the chance, she launched herself the remaining distance and grabbed the axe before the vile fiend could react.

Foolishly, the man lunged at Cinder—no doubt hoping he could wrestle the weapon from her grasp. Had he forgotten he spurted blood from his wound, that he was growing weaker by the moment? Without hesitation, she swung the ax at him again, watching as he bowed back to avoid the cutting blade before moving forward again. Seeing his crazed eyes, she pulled the axe back, changing the angle of her swing and then slashed at his filthy cock. Yes, she would deliver the final blow to his piece of shit dick that he'd nearly violated her with.

Blood shot out from his private region as the man howled in agony.

Die motherfucker.

Die a dickless monster.

Vomit rose in the back of her throat as her attacker fell to the floor. Cinder began to tremble so hard her teeth chattered. Tears nearly blinded her. He was dead! She'd killed a man!

Blood. So much blood. Blood everywhere. She'd killed another person. She'd killed a living breathing human.

No. She'd slayed the dragon. Just like in a fairytale.

The villain was dead.

Happily Ever After.

Happily Ever Fucking After.

12

"Are you all right?"

The sound of another man's voice brought tears to her eyes. Someone else was here! Help... a miracle... someone.

Cinder shifted her head to see a man looming in the shadows of the room. His silhouette exuded power. His deep voice possessed strength. This man could be another attacker... and yet, she didn't quite feel he was.

He approached Cinder with caution, his hands open to show he meant no harm. He acted as if he were walking toward a wounded wild animal. "Give me the axe. Everything's going to be okay." The shadowed man touched her forearm tentatively. Her head swirled in confusion. She looked down and saw that her bloodied hand still gripped the axe, scarlet now from blood she had spilled.

Murderer. She had become a murderer.

"He's dead and can't hurt you any longer." When Cinder didn't immediately hand over the weapon, he added, "I'm not going to hurt you. Just give me the axe." The gentleness of his voice somehow soothed her. Maybe foolishly, she handed it to him, looking him straight in the eyes. She knew at that very moment, she was in safe hands.

"How badly are you hurt?" he asked as he scanned for injuries.

She stared at her hands. Parts of her felt numb, while other parts radiated in pain. Cinder looked into his eyes and began to cry. He hesitated for a moment, but wrapped his arms around her beaten body. She clung to him as she sobbed, shaking violently. No longer able to stand, her knees buckled. The stranger gently lowered them both to the floor as he pulled away enough so he could look into her face.

"What are you doing here?" he hissed.

The harshness of the question confused her. Cinder sucked back the last sob, and quickly tried to regain her composure. "The Palace of Lazar is under attack by Jaden. We came here for safety, until reinforcements come."

"Who are *we*?"

"Women of the harem. We were split up so it would be harder to be captured. There's a bounty on our..." She paused, wishing she hadn't released the information.

"Why here? This commune was evacuated years ago. The resources have long dried up." Any sign of softness from this stranger became a distant memory.

"I don't know," she said. "We were told to go west and stop at the first commune. We did as we were told."

"Where are the rest of the women?" he asked, tension blanketing his face.

"I don't know. They ran when the man attacked."

"Why didn't you run?"

She shrugged. "I wanted to give them a head start. I thought more men might come."

The man stood and began to pace. "What's your name?"

"Cinder."

"And you say Jaden is attacking the palace? Word is, Jaden is conquering communes effortlessly and savagely. No survivors."

Cinder tried not to listen or believe. She wouldn't allow panic to set in on just a rumor. "The harem was sent out before the army of Jaden arrived. Lazar will not go down without a fight."

"What do you plan on doing now?" His tone sharpened with each question. "This commune's no place for you. It's dangerous."

She glanced up into his eyes. For the first time since leaving Donte, the feeling of hope took over. The foreign sensation caused her voice to quiver. "Are there people here? People who could help us?"

"The people who didn't migrate when the land dried up are just like the one who almost killed you. Is that what you're looking for?" His response stung like a slap to the face. He seemed annoyed that he even had to answer her question.

"What's your name?"

A muscle clenched in his jaw, forcing him to bite out the answer. "Nico. You didn't answer my question," he barked. "What do you plan on doing now?"

Her tongue stuck to the roof her mouth. Desperate for water, she swallowed hard against the lump that threatened to choke her. "I don't know. I need to find the others. I need to learn what might have happened to Lazar." She shut out the fear of the unknown with a shiver and folded her arms across her chest.

She glanced at the dead body lying face down

with a pool of blood beneath it. She couldn't stay here. The thought of it made her sick. An idea came to her that seemed about as crazy as coming into a death ravished commune with five women. But in her current situation, what did she have to lose?

Quickly, before she lost her nerve, she asked, "May I go with you? May I stay with you tonight?"

Slowly, he turned his head to look at her, his gaze flat and unblinking. "With me?" he repeated. "Have you lost your mind? How do you know I won't try to do the same thing that dead guy tried? Or worse?"

"You wouldn't." Cinder's head ached, so she pressed her hand against it to ease the pain. "You would've already made your move by now if that was your plan." When he didn't reply, she continued on. "It's almost dark. Just let me stay with you for one night and then I'll be on my way. Please."

Very deliberately, carefully, Nico spoke. "One night. Tomorrow morning you find the other women and leave. You continue to head further west. There's a farming commune about a two days walk. Are we clear?"

She hesitated. "I promise I'll be out of your hair first thing." She had no intention of making any promises she couldn't, or wouldn't, keep. She needed to get back to Donte or die trying. But she wasn't foolish enough to reveal that fact.

"Can you walk?" he asked as he held out his hand to her. "We need to get out of here."

13

Early the next morning, the sun shone brightly through the glass greenhouse Nico had brought her to last night. Cinder let out a slight groan and shielded her eyes from the bright rays. Her head still pounded from the night before. She squirmed from underneath Nico's protective embrace, something he must have done in his sleep. No way would he have done that awake... or would he?

She sat up and briefly scanned her surroundings, noticing broken pots and the remains of dead plants scattered around. Gardening tools hung on hooks and a pair of gloves sat on a wooden table. Leftover signs of human life caused Cinder to want to cry. She could envision someone gardening in here at one time.

Cinder bowed her head and hugged herself against the bitter cold as she turned her head and watched Nico still sleeping peacefully beside her.

She reached over and brushed away the few strands of his dark brown hair that fell over his eyes, allowing her fingertips to brush against his sun-kissed skin. It was odd touching a complete stranger, but she needed to do so to feel this was all real and not some kind of dark dream. She thought of all that happened last night, and knew that she was truly lucky he wasn't another attacker. She barely knew him, yet for some reason she felt she could trust him. Tears welled up at the corners of her eyes while she watched him sleep beneath the bright sun. She wondered if Donte was safe. Had he survived the attack? Was Nico correct when he said Jaden conquered all, and there would be no survivors? She shook the horrible thoughts away.

No. Donte was alive. He had to be alive. The prince? The guards? The rest of the harem? Everyone had to still be alive. They had to be.

Nico moved his head, moaning as he awoke. He opened his eyes and looked directly into Cinder's.

"Hey," he breathed. Pushing himself into a more upright position, he ran his fingers through his tousled hair while he let out a tired yawn and stretched out his muscles. "How long have you been awake?"

"Not long. My head and the aches in my body woke me up," she managed to say.

Nico scanned her face and head, no doubt taking stock of all her cuts and bruises from the attack.

"Are you cold?" he asked.

Cinder shrugged. She didn't want to lie, but she also didn't want to be a burden.

Concerned, he pulled Cinder close to him. "Come on," he said as he helped her up and wrapped the blanket they had shared last night around her shoulders. "Let's get you out of here."

Cinder held on to Nico, surprised by how drained she felt. She winced when a sharp pain shot through her head, causing her to almost black out. Without meaning to, she rested her head upon Nico's shoulder.

"I'm dizzy, Nico. I feel really weak," she admitted as she gazed up at him. Any strength she had prior seemed to have escaped her.

"You'll be fine," he reassured. "I'll make sure of it."

Cinder smiled and kept a tight hold of his arm. "Thank you," she murmured.

He paused briefly, then scooped her up into his arms. "We need to get some food in you."

She squinted against the sun as Nico carried her out on to the street, quickly making his way past a row of housing. Everywhere she looked, shuttered houses surrounded them. She let out an uneasy breath and grimaced upon noticing how run down and destroyed the structures had become. This was a far cry from the opulence of Lazar. She couldn't believe the condition of the dirty street Nico carried her down. It had been a while since she'd seen such filth, but she also knew that she would have to learn to accept it. At least until she found the rest of the women. Then she wasn't sure if she'd stay and wait for Donte as he ordered, or if she should go back to Lazar and find him.

Nico stopped in front of a rundown building about a mile away from where they had spent the night.

"This is the place we're going to be staying in?" Cinder asked nervously as she glanced up at the building, taking in the once elegant façade beat down by apocalyptic elements that had ended everything. It looked like it once belonged to a leader or wealthy resident of the commune.

"Yes," he said, looking down at her with a worried expression. "It's not as nice as I'd like to take you, but we need to get off the street and get you inside. I know it's secure."

"Okay," she said, feeling safer than she had since leaving Lazar.

Nico led her up the stone steps and through the front door. The wallpaper was peeling. A horrible stench filled the air. Cinder hoped it wasn't death and there weren't any dead bodies lying around. Dust and cobwebs engulfed the front room, a sad contrast to the place of grandeur she imagined it had once been. Mankind had not stepped foot through these doors for quite some time. Cinder flinched when she noticed cockroaches scurrying across the floor, which only caused her to press against Nico's chest even further. Nico glanced down at her and gave a reassuring smile as he carried her towards the stairs.

The inside of the bedroom they entered was surprisingly impressive, with its antiques and brocade covered furniture. Along the back wall, Cinder took in the fireplace looming over a large canopy bed. A thick layer of dust had settled everywhere, but the room seemed inviting. Nico walked over to a red velvet couch and gently set Cinder down. He went to a closet and pulled out a blanket and pillow. Without saying a word, he came back over, positioned the pillow behind Cinder's head, and covered her with the blanket.

He rubbed his palms together. "First thing's first. Let's get a fire going and warm up this room."

Cinder pulled the blanket up to her chin, shivering. "I think that's a great idea." She couldn't help but smile as she watched Nico quickly go about starting a fire. He struck the flint and stone with expertise, feeding the small curl of smoking dry tinder until he soon had a small blaze going. Although she still shivered beneath the blanket, just listening to the crackle and pop of the friendly little fire made the room seem much warmer.

"I'm going to see about finding us something to eat," Nico said as he wiped his hands on his pants and stepped outside.

There seemed to be enough wood for a few days, she thought as she examined the woodpile. No wonder Nico chose this place. It would keep them warm for awhile. Might even last a week. Cinder grinned. She could find Maysa and the rest of the harem, and stay here for a while.

The doorknob rattled and then the door opened. Nico juggled a tray in one hand while he pulled the door closed with his other hand. "There's a large pantry in the kitchen," he said. "It was pretty well stocked with cans. I made us some beans and corn."

Cinder's stomach growled, reminding her that she hadn't eaten much in a couple of days. No doubt adding to her weakened condition.

Nico set the tray on the couch next to her. Along with plates, there were also two glasses of red wine. Her mouth suddenly dry, she picked up one of the glasses and sipped the delicious liquid.

"Wine is one of the few things that actually gets better with age," he said with a grin.

"I can't believe you found wine!" She reached now for the fork, shoveling a mouthful of beans into her mouth, the flavor dancing across her tongue.

"Wine is easy to come by," he replied matter-of-factly.

"What?" She must have heard him wrong. Or the wine already had her ears buzzing.

"I've gotten pretty good at being a scavenger," he said with obvious pride and complete acceptance. "Survival is a tricky thing."

After about thirty minutes of eating and drinking in silence, Cinder couldn't keep quiet any longer. "Nico?"

Nico settled onto the couch on the other side of the tray. "Yes?"

"Thank you."

He lifted his fingers to her right temple and pushed back a lock of her blood-soaked hair. Lightly, he ran his fingertip along a cut on her head. "We just need to get you back on your feet. That bastard could have killed you."

"I know," she breathed, as the realization almost made her ill. "I've never killed anyone before."

He leaned over the tray and cupped her chin. "You had no choice. You shouldn't have been in the commune to begin with. There are some people remaining here, but it's not what you think. It's ruthless. Deadly. Those who remain are some of the worst examples of mankind."

"Then why are you here?"

"I'm stockpiling. I have a bigger plan in store. Trust me, when I can, I'll leave and never look back." He took a large gulp of wine and poured both of them some more.

Her temple pounded now, but she was trying her best to hide it from Nico. He had worried enough. "What plan? Where are you going? Are you going alone?"

He patted her leg. "Another story for another time. You need to finish eating so you can get some rest. I still plan on making you leave this commune as soon as you are able."

"Why didn't you leave with everyone else?"

He shrugged. "And go where? The world is drying up one commune at a time. I'm done being a nomad. I need to find a way to survive with what Mother Nature has left us."

"Scavenging off ruins?"

"Finish eating," he pressed.

"Maybe you don't have to be alone. Maybe we found each other for a reason." Her eyes were growing heavy. Exhaustion and wine were a deadly mix.

"That's the wine talking," Nico said, smiling.

Her face flushed. "The prince will get Lazar back," she said, defending her stance. "You could come back with me and the rest of the harem. They'll be grateful that you helped us return. There's a reason we met. Maybe it's because you are supposed to be with us all along."

"Eat," he said simply.

"I'm serious," Cinder continued to push.

"Maybe you're right," he said.

Cinder stared at him in surprise. She hadn't expected him to admit to it so easily.

"There was a reason we found each other," he added. "So you don't get raped and killed."

Tears of frustration threatened to escape Cinder's eyes. Why was the man so stubborn? "You aren't being honest. You don't want to live as a bottom feeder," she said.

His jaw clenched. "Are you all done?" he asked as he removed the tray.

"I need to find the girls," she slurred. "And I need a plan."

"It's time you get some rest. I'm pretty sure you have a concussion and your body took a beating and needs to recoup," he directed, as he picked her up and carried her to the bed.

She closed her eyes and sighed. "They're out there alone right now."

"Cinder—"

She pressed her fingers over his lips. "I know, I know. Get some rest. I will. But promise me something."

"If it means you finally quieting your mind and body to heal... anything," he teased.

"That if I fall asleep, you'll be here when I wake up."

He pulled the blanket up to her chin and tucked her in. "I promise."

14

Cinder let out a shuddering breath as she stared at her reflection in the mirror. Gaunt would be an understatement. She hadn't realized how filthy she was. Grateful for the basin of water she found in the bathroom, she smiled knowing Nico had found it somewhere for her. It wasn't the cleanest, and certainly not drinkable, but it would make do to clean herself with.

Nico was asleep in the other room, so Cinder was careful not to wake him, even though she wanted to thank him profusely. The man confused her. One moment he was closed and short, and the next he was devoted and kind.

Her silk wrap was almost black with grime. Bloodstains covered most of the fabric. Suddenly, she was desperate to remove every inch of the item, attempting to erase the horrible memory of nearly being raped. She shed her clothes and let them fall to a disgusting heap on the floor. Wrapping herself in a towel, she decided to figure out her clothing situation later. For now, she just wanted to feel clean.

She stared in the mirror once again. Her once bouncy waves hung heavy and were caked with dried blood, a mixture of hers and the man she'd killed. She let out a sigh and picked up a washcloth as she proceeded to give herself a sponge bath. Once she was through with her body and hair, she went about trying to wash her clothes. The process took longer than expected; using up what little energy she had left. She hung her clothes over a hook to dry, walked over to the sofa and sat down, exhausted. She leaned back against her seat and closed her eyes for a brief moment, before taking in a deep breath and allowing herself to relax. Feeling an odd sensation, she opened her eyes to find Nico staring at her with annoyance painted all over his face.

"You shouldn't be out of bed," he said as he crossed his arms across his chest.

"What? I...uh..." Cinder couldn't get a clear sentence out. "I needed to clean the blood off. I'm fine."

His eyebrow shot up. "Really? You don't look

fine to me. You should be resting and instead you overdid it and pushed too far." He reached for a blanket and placed it over her nude shoulders.

Cinder suddenly remembered that she was sitting in nothing but a dingy terry cloth towel, and barely one at that. She blushed. "I was dirty. I couldn't stand it anymore."

Nico leaned in and examined the wound on her head. "You should have let me help you." His eyes swept over her towel, resting where the fabric scarcely covered the top of her thighs. "Why don't you get dressed?" he suggested. "I found some clothes last night while you were sleeping. They're in the closet. I'm pretty sure they'll fit."

Cinder gaped at him as he brushed past her and sat down. He flopped down on the sofa and shot her an expectant look. "Go on," he prompted.

She blinked, surprised that once again, Nico had thought of everything. She got up and headed for the bathroom. Except for Donte, she had never experienced someone this "take charge". There was something about Nico that made her feel comfortable. She had just met him, and yet, she didn't want to leave his side.

When she stepped back into the main room a few minutes later, she wore a pair of black pants, a loose white blouse and a careful expression. It had been a while since she had worn anything beside silk or satin. Something about it felt like a betrayal to Donte and the palace. What would the mistresses say if they saw her now?

Nico nodded his approval. "You look really nice. I'm glad the clothes fit."

"Yes, thank you. I guess you've really mastered the scavenger thing, huh?"

He smiled. "You have no idea." Nico stood up and reached for her hand, pulling her to sit back down on the couch. "How are you feeling?"

"Much better. I guess I needed the food and rest more than I knew." She looked down at her hands, avoiding his eyes. "I suppose I can leave you alone now." Her heart heavy with sadness, she could barely say the words.

"Are you heading to the farming commune?"

"Um... well... I don't know. I'll figure it out." She wanted to tell him about Donte, but decided it would be revealing too much. "Don't worry about me."

"I figured you'd say that," he said dryly. "Which is why I've decided to escort you out of this commune myself. I'm going to make sure you're safe and sound and far from this forsaken place."

Cinder was about to nod in false agreement, then glanced at him sharply, clear defiance in her eyes. She studied him for a moment, figuring out how to go into battle with him. She had no desire to fight with the man... she had a feeling he would win. But she had to convince him of her idea.

Finally, she said, "No."

Nico didn't bother hiding his displeasure. "It wasn't a suggestion. You're going if it means me throwing you over my shoulder and carrying you the whole way kicking and screaming. You *will* be safe, whether you like it or not."

She crossed her arms over her chest, an action she knew would poke at his temper even more. If it were Donte, she would be under the leather lash in an instant for such behavior. He glared, causing her to avert her eyes.

"No to leaving *yet*," she elaborated. "I'll go wherever you want to go, but I need to find the rest of the women first. They're my friends." She knew she had a better chance at staying alive and finding them if she stuck with Nico. "Please help me."

A sigh escaped his lips. "Cinder. Have you lost your mind? It's dangerous here. Didn't last night prove that to you? Hopefully the women ran right out of the commune and back to the desert. If they had any common sense, they would have. It's too dangerous for you to even stay another day."

"Then protect me."

"Cinder—" he started.

"You," she cut in. "I want you to protect me,

Nico, and I want you to help me find my friends. I won't settle for anything else."

Nico began pacing the room. He stopped in front of her with his hands on his hips. "You aren't calling the shots here. I am." His voice boomed even though he never yelled.

Evidently, she was a huge masochist. Maybe pathetic, too, because she was willing to beg if that's what it came down to. This man showed no signs of wanting her in his life. Hell, he was trying to get rid of her, and yet... yet, she would do anything to have him stay and help her. She owed it to the women to see that they were safe.

"Okay, call the shots. I'll do whatever you want. Just don't ask me to leave without knowing for sure the women aren't here." And so, the begging began.

"You can't be everyone's savior. You need to look out for yourself. We are alone in this ruthless world," Nico said, his voice coming out gruff.

Cinder raised one eyebrow. A part of her knew he didn't mean what he said, otherwise he wouldn't have helped her. She thought it best not to contradict him. "I'm not alone. There are people I need to find. I have friends. Surely you can understand that."

"Having friends will get you killed. Look what just happened to you. You stayed behind to fight off that man so your friends could get away. If you'd run and worried about your own ass, you wouldn't have come close to being raped or been almost beaten to death. You need to leave before it happens again," he said bluntly.

"I won't leave this place unless I'm positive they aren't here any longer. I'm scared! I'm terrified! I feel like a scared little girl afraid of the dark. I can't take it anymore! But I would rather risk my life, than walk away feeling I abandoned them. I'd rather my body die than my soul."

Something in his brown eyes softened. "Staying here will be harder than you think." To her shock, his voice suddenly cracked as he added, "But I won't make you leave your friends."

Her breath caught in her throat. For the first time since they met, there was genuine emotion in his voice. A hint of sorrow. A note of compassion. And she couldn't be certain, but a flicker of understanding in his eyes.

Swallowing, she murmured, "Please. I won't be a burden. I'll help. I'll contribute."

"I'm not an easy man," he said flatly. "I'll have expectations."

Cinder nodded eagerly. "Whatever they are... I swear I'll do."

A heavy silence fell between them. Nico glanced around the room for a moment, as if the furniture would help him make up his mind. And then his gaze landed directly on hers.

Finally, he said, "All right."

A ray of hope exploded from her chest. "You mean it? Yes?"

He let out a breath. "On a couple of conditions."

"Yes, yes! I told you, anything." Cinder wanted to jump up and down and clap her hands together in glee.

"I wouldn't get too excited if I were you. You may not like the conditions."

Her heart skipped. Was he going to demand sex? She would never betray Donte. Her body belonged to him. "What are they?"

"I'm in charge. I will lead us to the best of my ability, but you need to allow me to lead at all times."

She nodded in agreement.

"I expect your constant respect. But I will make damn sure I earn it."

She nodded again.

"I need you to trust in me. Trust that from this point on you are mine to protect. I don't take that lightly."

Cinder paused and studied Nico's face. "I can do that. I'm trained in submission as a member of the harem."

Nico grinned. "We'll see about that."

"And if I don't? Will you leave?" Cinder hated knowing that the threat of that would always loom over them.

He shook his head. "No. I stand by my word and commitments. But this is not a democracy. Just know that I lead, you follow."

Cinder sat in silence, taking it all in.

"Those are my conditions. Take them or leave them."

His conditions didn't seem awful. And frankly, she didn't care what he demanded. She would do anything to stay with Nico and figure a way to find Donte and everyone else.

"Deal," she announced.

He offered his hand to make it official. "Deal."

Slowly, she lifted her hand to his, letting him grip it. Solid. Strong. His touch reminded her of Donte.

Please, Donte, be alive.
Be alive.

15

They both fell silent, listening to the sounds around them. Cinder feared their silence, feared the hushed stillness more than anything else. She hated it.

"Why are you so quiet?" Nico asked. His breath whispered against her neck, the heat tore her in half. She was afraid of the commune, afraid of the darkness that loomed around them, unsure of the man she leaned against for warmth, and yet here was the only place she wanted to be. She had to remain in this nightmare in order to turn it into a dream. She couldn't run. She couldn't hide. She was the leader in charge, and her duty was to save the harem. But she couldn't help but feel she had failed them all. Donte would be so disappointed.

She shrugged her shoulders.

Nico left the subject alone. The wind howled through the alleyways in the distance, a fear-provoking sound that made her heart skip and her body quiver. She disliked the night. Even in the calm, darkness held evil which crept down her neck and gave Cinder the chills.

"I don't want you to be afraid. I'll keep you safe."

"Do you think the girls are out there?" Cinder asked. "What about the men you speak of? Are they out there watching... waiting?"

"They're far enough away, and they won't come near us unless provoked."

"What if they feel provoked?"

"We have nothing to offer them right now." He repositioned his arm to have a stronger hold on her. "We'll search for the girls at dawn."

His strong arms engulfed her in a brief, reassuring hug, before releasing so he could tend to the fire. His hands gripped the iron poker, their power and strength mesmerized her, and as much as she wanted to fight the fact, Cinder enjoyed being with him. She should be searching for the girls, but right now, she relished the warmth and safety of Nico.

"I really like this room. It makes me feel safe."

Nico nodded as he repositioned the smoldering wood." I remember reading about a place like this once when I was a young boy."

Grabbing a few pieces of fresh wood, he added them to the fire. When he caught Cinder's smile, his face blushed in a bright shade of red. "Sorry, stupid memory I guess," he mumbled.

"Why say sorry? Memories are all we have left now."

Nico stood and walked to the window, gazing down to the empty street below.

"So, why did you join the harem?" he asked, never taking his gaze away from the window.

"I wanted a better life. Like you, I was tired of the nomadic way of life." Cinder looked down into her hands. "Being part of the harem is a vibrant, colorful existence. Much better than the dull drabness of desert sand."

"Why? Why give your body to someone?" he asked.

"I wanted the power to be able to do so. I wanted the freedom to decide my fate."

"Are the stories true? The sexual tales every man fantasizes about? Were you a part of it all?"

Though she didn't know for a fact all of it to be true since she had yet to meet with the prince, Cinder nodded. Not feeling shame in the slightest. "All the tales are true. Lust, debauchery, taboo, dominance and submission

"Do you miss it?"

Cinder smiled. "No. I crave it. It was everything I ever pictured."

"Sitting here, beaten, lost, scared. Is that what you pictured?"

"I thought I'd be safe." Cinder swallowed the sorrow threatening to consume her. "What about you?"

Nico turned to stare at her. "What about me?"

"Why didn't you leave in search of a better commune? How long have you been here?"

"It doesn't matter."

Cinder huffed. "So I have to answer your questions, but you don't have to answer mine?"

"Not a democracy, remember?" He turned back to the window and stared off into the blackness, lost in thought, and not the reaction to her comments that she had hoped for.

"Nico, I didn't mean to be nosey. It's just—" Cinder bit her tongue as soon as she saw his expression. The conversation needed to end, now. "Will you tell me about the people who are still here?"

He sat down next to her. "They are out for blood. Our only hope is to go where these people wouldn't want to follow."

"People? How many people are we talking about?" Maybe Donte was with them, searching for her.

"More like monsters. These *people* who remained, we want nothing to do with."

"But they can't be all bad? We aren't. How do you know?"

"I'm not willing to risk finding out." He leaned in and nudged his shoulder into hers. His playful act made Cinder's stomach flip. "Trust me, okay?"

"I... I... do," she stuttered, trying to steady her voice.

"Good." Nico stroked her arm with his soft fingers, and chills ran down her spine. The touch made her feel wrong. Her heart belonged to Donte, yet the comforting touch of Nico was welcomed.

Cinder reached for her glass of wine, but froze when she heard dogs barking in the distance.

"Nico–"

"Shh." Nico placed his finger to his lip. The dogs sounded closer now. "I'll be right back. You stay here."

"What? Where are you going?"

Nico extinguished the fire as fast as he could and blew out the candles. He quickly pulled the curtains shut. "Stay here and don't open the door for anyone. Do you understand?"

"I'm coming with you."

"No," he snapped in a whisper. "You'll stay here like I said!"

"I'm going with you," she insisted. "You aren't leaving me here."

His expression and tone told Cinder he was furious, but evidently he didn't have time to argue. He reached for her hand harshly and led her through the door, down the stairs, and out to the street. Running closer and closer to the bellowing howls, they slowed their pace and kept their attention on their surroundings, searching for any sign of movement. They changed direction a few times before Nico stopped and knelt beside a rusted dumpster. Cinder hunched down beside him and squinted in the darkness. Suddenly, a woman ran past several feet from where they hid. It was Maysa!

Maysa screamed at the vicious canines nipping at her legs. The fear in her voice made the hair on Cinder's neck stand up and impending doom run down her spine. Within seconds, Maysa screamed again as the dogs grabbed a hold of her ripped silk wrap and drove her into the ground, biting into her limbs as if she was the last meal they would ever receive. Cinder lunged forward to help her, but Nico grabbed her and pinned her to the ground next to the metal garbage bin.

"Don't move," he whispered.

"Let me–"

"You'll get yourself killed. Don't fucking move," he commanded.

Cinder struggled with him as he covered her mouth with his hand. Footsteps ran past them and a man called out, evoking horrifying, unimaginable fear. Cinder trembled under Nico's weight. He lay on top of her, his arms wrapped around her, his face closer than ever before.

"I won't let anything happen to you," he whispered. "Remain silent, or we are all dead."

Wrenching her head free of his hand, she pleaded, "We've got to help her. Please help her."

"It's too late. She's dead... or will be."

She closed her eyes and squeezed him tight. She prayed for this nightmare to end.

"Get them off of me! Help! Stop them!" Maysa begged in terror and pure agony as the dogs tore her flesh from the bones. Her screams for mercy were the worst sound that Cinder had ever heard in her life.

"We gave you a chance to put your harem charms to good use," the man shouted, and released a maniacal laugh. "You foolishly refused and now will be nothing but dog food."

Cinder couldn't close her eyes. Even though she knew. She knew what she would see. She tensed and dug her nails into Nico's skin. He pressed his body into hers, shoving them closer into the hidden shadows of the dumpster.

With one quick motion, one of the dogs ripped Maysa's throat with its bloody teeth. Barking, growling, and the sounds of gurgling blood spurting from Maysa's neck filled the air.

"Let's get out of here," one of the men said.

"We can bring the dogs back here tomorrow to feed them breakfast," another said.

Cinder heard Maysa gasping. The dogs hadn't killed her. Just feet from where they hid, lay her friend writhing in pain and facing death.

"Don't move an inch," Nico whispered. Suddenly a cold, wet dog nose pressed against Cinder's arm. She froze, holding her breath and closing her eyes, fighting the urge to yank her arm away from the dog. The dog sniffed around Nico and her, and the more she tried to hold her breath, the more Cinder's lungs struggled for air. Slowly, she buried her face into Nico's neck, waiting to die.

Having no real interest in them, the dog finally left. Cinder shivered as she lay on the cold ground. Nico reached up and clutched the back of her head. How he maintained a steady breath, she didn't know. Her heart raced, and she couldn't stop shaking no matter how hard she tried to make herself. Nico placed a soft, reassuring kiss on her cheek, and moments later, heavy boot steps ran past them, disappearing in the distance with the two large dogs. Cinder struggled to move, but Nico still wouldn't let her go.

"Wait," he whispered. "They aren't out of my line of sight yet."

Seconds seemed like hours as she lay underneath him. Maysa drowned in her own blood on the other side of the dumpster, each painful breath stabbing at Cinder's ears. Nico finally rose and released her as she ran to the dying woman's side. Still alive, but with only minutes left, she inhaled in search for life that didn't exist. Death was near. And by the looks of Maysa's ravaged and half-eaten body, death would be merciful.

"Everything's going to be all right," Cinder said, kneeling down beside her. "I won't let anyone hurt you again, I promise."

Maysa clawed at Cinder, crying and gasping. The only comfort Cinder could give her was to cradle her head and stroke her forehead. Her body jerked, blood gushed out her neck as well as from the other torn flesh of her limbs, and the bloodstains on Cinder's clothing grew with every second. Death blanketed her.

"You're going to be okay," Cinder said, loathing her own words. Arteries had been ripped open by the jaws of the vicious dogs, and blood flowed from them freely. Maysa was moments from death, and this was all Cinder could offer. "Those men had nothing over you. You faced them head on with courage and grace. You are a proud woman, and I will tell everyone how brave you are."

Maysa's eyes widened and she wheezed through failed breaths. She tried to speak, but her own blood strangled her. She only had minutes left, if not seconds.

"Relax. Just relax. It won't be long until you get to see all your loved ones again. They'll be there waiting. They're waiting for you. Just close your eyes and relax." She refused to allow Maysa see her sob, so held in the need to fall apart right there and then. "And I'll save the others. Don't worry. I'll find them and save them."

Cinder wasn't sure how much of her words Maysa heard. No one should have to suffer toward death alone and afraid. Cinder would not allow her to die without a friendly face holding her hand.

Maysa opened her mouth to try to speak again and blood gushed out as she grabbed Cinder's hands, shaking with a grip of pure panic. She faced the fear of death.

What did it feel like to know you were going to die, and there was nothing you could do about it?

"You're safe now. You're safe now," Cinder repeated her words, rocking on her knees with her dying friend's head in her lap until she took her final rattled breath. Cinder set down her head, rose, and stumbled to the alley wall, mourning the loss of a woman she couldn't save. Grieving someone she had grown to love. Her lungs heaved, unable to breathe through her sobs.

"We couldn't have saved her," Nico whispered as he approached her.

Cinder leaned against the cold stone wall for support, covered in blood and lacking any sanity in her body to talk. She bit her lip, shook her head, and turned away from him, burying her face in her bloody hands. Pure madness was setting in as she actually considered bashing her own head into the wall over and over to put herself out of her misery.

Hell.

She lived in absolute Hell.

This was not a world worth living in.

If this world allowed a sweet and innocent woman to be nearly eaten alive by what should be docile pets... she wanted to leave it just as Maysa had.

"I know that wasn't easy to witness." He paused for a moment. "Look at me when I'm speaking to you, please." Cinder removed her hands and faced him, but couldn't look into his eyes.

Nico continued, his tone fiercely disapproving. "I told you to stay. I demanded it. But you were too stubborn. Too stubborn to listen. How am I supposed to keep you with me if you won't listen? How can I know this won't happen again?" His words were more of a statement than a question.

"She was my friend! She was a human being who didn't deserve to die like that! Dogs tore her to shreds while men just watched on in delight." She glanced down at her bloody hands. "While we watched as well."

"No, she didn't deserve it. And you were seconds from suffering the same fate. Your attempt at bravery can't be confused with foolishness!"

"We should have done something. If you hadn't have held me back..."

"Do you know what they would have done to you if they found us? They would have just killed me. But do you know what they would have done to you before killing you?"

"Yes, Nico, I know exactly what they would do, and death would be a blessing in comparison. I have been living in this fucked up world just like you. I know how ruthless men have become. I fucking know, all right? I know."

"Do you know I would have died tonight trying to protect you?"

"Yes."

"I don't believe you do, Cinder. Do you know the predicament you put me in? This new world we're in is tough enough without me having to worry about taking care of your ass!"

"Nico, I'm sorry. But she was such a good person. How could this happen? How could anyone—"

"Do you believe me now? Do you see why we have to leave this commune? If the women are still here... they're most likely dead."

"Yes," Cinder whispered. "I see that now. But I just can't leave them if they are still here. How can we be sure?"

Nico opened his mouth to speak, but paused for a few seconds as if searching for the perfect words. "I've seen worse. I've seen things and experienced stuff I would never wish on you." He took a deep breath and continued. "I'll protect you, Cinder. I'll make sure you're safe from it all. I gave you my word that I would. But you have to let me lead. I'm the commander in this fucked up war. Not you. You have to trust in what I say, and never question me again. I promise you I'll die trying. But I ask you to never fight me again. I don't do teams well. I've survived this long by worrying about me alone. I'm a man of my word, but I'm also not a fool. I need you to also not act like one."

Cinder simply nodded.

Nico's expression softened. "Are you going to be okay?"

"No."

"I'm sorry you had to see that." Nico reached for her hand and pulled her into an embrace.

He held her as she cried, stroking her hair softly. He stepped backwards away from her, swiping at the tears streaming down Cinder's face. Unable to stand any longer, Cinder dropped to her knees and sobbed out his name. "Donte. Please help me find Donte."

Nico held her tight and stroked her hair. "Who's Donte?"

"The man I love. He's alive. I know he's alive. Please, Nico. Please!" The sobs choked her, causing her words to come out in gasps. "I know I should have told you about him. I shouldn't have tried to hide anything, but... He told me to find the nearest commune and wait. I tried. I tried so hard."

Nico nodded against her hair. "Okay, Cinder. Okay. Just calm down. You aren't making a lot of sense."

"I was supposed to be in charge of protecting them when we left the palace. He thought I knew the desert better than any of them, which was true. He put me in charge of the harem's safety." She sobbed even louder. "I failed him. I failed them."

"Shh, calm down. You haven't failed anyone."

Then she heard the words. The words that changed everything.

"Don't move! Don't fucking move! You two stay where you are."

Cinder looked at Nico in panic. She saw the look in Nico's eyes. The look of a man about to die. Then there were men beating on him...

There was a fierce punch to her face.

Darkness.

16

Cinder stood third in line to be raped by beasts cloaked as men. General Rhys, the leader of Jaden, loomed ahead as he wiped off his sword, which was soaking in blood. The wailing cries of terrified harem girls not ready to meet with the sharp edge of a blade echoed against the backdrop of the brutal desert.

She had found the harem.

Or the harem had found her.

Actually... Jaden had found them both.

United.

United in Hell.

Jaden had also managed to find another one of the groups. The women who had been led by Mistress Tula had also been captured by Jaden. They too stood in this line of doom.

They stood in line to be taken by these men. They had no choice but to give up their virtue or suffer the same fate of the first girl who refused to willingly sacrifice her body to Rhys.

In the corner of her eye, Cinder caught a glimpse of her friend—limbs slack, throat slit, tossed onto a pile of sand. This brave woman had refused to be taken by General Rhys and lost her life because of it. Cinder wished she, too, could be undaunted by the face of death. But her shaking body and labored breath revealed her paralyzing fear. She knew her body belonged to Donte... but she didn't want to die.

The Jaden soldiers barked their orders to the crying women, ordering them all to remove their clothes. No amount of sobs, pleas, or wails softened the stone-cold hearts of the soldiers. And each time a woman hesitated or tried to conceal her body, the distinct crack of a fist to flesh sounded in the sweltering desert air.

A gaunt-faced goon, slightly bemused, gave an order. "Strip for your new leader!" He walked up and down the row of women and sneered. "Where is your precious Palace of Lazar now? I don't see the prince here to rescue you." An evil laugh stopped his speech before he continued. "When we are done with you all, you will be nothing but used up whores. No prince will come in on his white horse and save a dirty whore."

The soldier's depraved disregard of women reminded Cinder of her birth commune of Briar. She'd thought it had been ruthless, but nothing compared to what she was now witnessing of this Jaden army. Once a year, Briar rounded up their young women and auctioned them off like cattle to the highest bidder.. Luckily for Cinder, she'd fled the commune before she could be owned by anyone. Her life changed that day, for the better once she finally found the Palace of Lazar. Being part of the harem of Lazar, although a bit frightening at first, proved to be the answer to her prayers. She'd become safe, protected, nurtured... everything she could ask for—until the day Jaden had arrived and conquered. Now she lived in a nightmare, far worse than anything she'd endured at Briar. The commune of Jaden possessed a thirst for power that fueled an evil she'd never known existed.

General Rhys, a man who wore nothing more than heavy boots and all black clothing, became the leader of the Jaden army. He spoke with such vile in his scratchy voice. "Don't worry, ladies. We promise to give you back to the prince. But not until you are nothing but desert dirt to him." His words made the soldiers laugh and the women cry harder. "You should all be angry with your beloved prince. He sent his precious harem off to the dangerous desert to fend for themselves. Did he really think you would all be safe?" He crossed his arms and studied the naked women shivering before him. "If I were you, I would blame *him* for your misfortune. Not me."

He was right. The prince, Donte and the guards should have never sent the harem away. Sending them out to a barren landscape in the hope that they would find safety had always screamed of insanity to Cinder. She had cried, even begged to remain in the palace. She would rather have taken her chances there than be split up like Donte dictated.

The Jaden soldiers had found them.

They came out of nowhere, and in a surprise attack, snatched Cinder and the harem, holding them hostage just as Donte had originally feared. Now they would all be raped and maybe killed to send a message to the Prince of Lazar. Cinder readied her mind for the inevitable.

The next woman in line, no older than eighteen, crawled forth, her bound hands making the motion awkward and slow. Smudges of grime and sweat smeared her once porcelain skin. One of the watching soldiers lifted her to her feet to stand before General Rhys.

"Don't crawl like an animal. Stand before the general. Well... at least until he fucks you like an animal," the soldier spat.

Mad laughter echoed all around them. The woman stood fully upright, straightened her shoulders, and spat in the soldier's face. Pride and fear mixed as Cinder watched the woman stand with renewed indignant courage. "Kill me. I will never let that poor excuse of a cock enter me," she declared.

With tears in her eyes, Cinder couldn't help but watch the proud woman face the devil in the sand. The only saving grace was that she never saw it coming—the second they slit her throat. Horrified, Cinder hooked her arm against her mouth to stifle a scream. Soon afterward, it was Cinder's turn.

"Next!"

Cinder didn't budge. She refused. Her body stiff, she couldn't move an inch.

A disfigured eye leaned in, inches from Cinder's sunburned cheek. "Must I repeat myself?" the man asked, raising a bushy brow. His breath smelled like rotten flesh and spittle formed in the corners of his lips.

Cinder's heart gushed blood to her face, not certain if one wrong word would be her last. Could she be brave and die without giving a part of her she only wanted to ever share with Donte? Should she just allow Rhys to take her? It could all be over in moments. Cinder started to cry. She was supposed to have been their leader, but somewhere along the line had become broken. Maybe it was watching Maysa be torn to shreds, maybe it was knowing Nico had been beaten to death. Maybe it was knowing all these harem women would be raped or killed before her. Regardless...

She was broken.

She turned her head to search the other girls' faces for an answer. They all stared back at her, with terror in their eyes. It wasn't until she saw Mistress Tula, their old disciplinarian from a day that seemed long gone, that she knew what she had to do. Mistress Tula made eye contact and softly shook her head. Silently, she was instructing Cinder to not let the man touch her. Could she die with honor as the two other women before her had?

General Rhys nodded at his soldier. "Kill her." His command was quick and simple.

His henchman placed the knife at her neck, but his arm stopped just as it pinched Cinder's skin. The sickly looking man staggered back, gasping for air and fell to his knees.

Bewildered, Cinder craned her neck, looking straight into his once life-filled eyes. Was he dead?

She shuffled forward at a shout in the open

desert. Cinder clutched her nude body, peering out through her scraggly, matted hair. Men with axes, swords, and knives rushed out from behind concrete rubble, moving in a wave across the sand.

"Goddamn, Lazar..." General Rhys cursed as he pulled his sword from his belt, ready to take a stand.

The Jaden men charged, leaving the harem girls alone in the sand. A haze of death, screams, and bloodshed blurred around them. Cinder kneeled on the ground, huddled with the other women, and wished for the best. Helpless due to the ties around their hands, the women could do nothing but watch the battle around them.

Cinder then saw a man running toward her as she sat on her knees. Briskly, he brandished his knife and ripped through her flimsy restraints. The crippling fear she felt was only an afterthought as she looked up into the man's rich blue eyes. She remembered those eyes.

Oh God, was she delirious?

Had madness completely taken over her mind?

Donte? Donte was here to save them. When she tried to stand, he grabbed her frail arms and pulled her to her feet.

"We need to cut them all loose," he shouted. "Get them out of here now!"

General Rhys and his Jaden army, retreated

back into the desert abyss. It was hard for Cinder to believe anyone would save her—save any of them. As the other men hacked free the captured women, she pressed her hand on Donte's sleeve. She honestly didn't know if she could remain standing. A faint darkness threatened to overcome her as a ringing buzzed in her ears.

"You saved me," she said, her voice quiet and grateful. "They were going to kill me. Kill us all."

"You look pretty damned shaken," he replied. "Did they hurt you badly? Are you able to walk?"

She tried to take a step and her legs buckled underneath her. In that exact moment, he reeled her in, close to his chest. The heat of being held so tightly made the skin prickle on her arms and legs. Being bundled like that eased her violent trembling and allowed her to breathe at a normal cadence.

"Cinder, I need to look at these bruises."

Cinder stared in silence as he examined her condition. He examined the gash on her ribs that she somehow got along her torturous adventure.

"Are you in a lot of pain?"

She shook her head.

His nose flared with his deep breaths. "Did they rape you?" he asked calmly, but his expression revealed a hint of anger.

She shook her head. Cinder's heart pounded in

her chest, lacking the strength and courage to relive the awful attack. He wasn't listening anyway. His head needed to be calm, not hot with anger.

"Donte, please forget about the bruises."

"Tell me what happened, now." The order was firm and unwavering.

"They lunged at me, grabbed me by my neck, and threw me to the ground. I tried to run away from them, but they caught me and hit me repeatedly. I struggled to fight them. Nico did his best to protect me, but there were too many of them and they overpowered us."

"Who's Nico?" Donte asked.

"A man who tried to help me, but... they got him too."

Donte nodded. "Go on."

"They choked me, punched me several times, and then things got blurry. I tried to fight as hard as I could, but things went black and..." Tears burned her eyes. "Then more men came..."

Donte kept examining Cinder's body, his fingers tracing along the bruises across her neck, chest, and the wound at her ribcage. The pain in his eyes broke her heart.

"I should have been there."

"Donte, you couldn't have stopped them, and you couldn't have saved Nico. Just get me out of here." She glanced around at all the dead bodies and didn't want to breathe the air of death any longer.

"I will kill them for what they did to you."

Cinder looked at Donte with tears cascading. "I'm so scared, Donte. I'm terrified of what's to come. What happens now?" Cinder pointed to the distance behind him. "Jaden's army is out there, and they'll keep killing until they take over all the communes. They're ruthless, and the desert is making them worse."

"We'll figure it out," Donte whispered. "I am sorry, Cinder. I had no idea this would happen. I would have never allowed this if I had felt your life would be in danger. I thought you and the rest of the harem would be safe by splitting up."

"You had no way of knowing," she mumbled against his chest.

"I should have been here to protect you." Guilt flooded his expression. "To fight alongside this man you speak of, Nico."

Cinder shook her head. "No. I'm glad you weren't there. There were too many of them, and you would have died, just like Nico." She pulled away and stood up, wrapping her arms around her still shaking torso. "But everything happens for a reason, Donte. You're here now. And right now I need you."

Running footsteps approached as one of Lazar's

men flew up and stood before them. "Sir, it's all clear."

"How many dead?" Donte's breath was warm against the side of her face as his embrace remained strong around her small frame.

"Two harem girls and seven men in battle. We killed ten of their men before they ran off like cowards."

"Help these women get dressed and covered," he ordered. "Make sure everyone is taken care of and ready to travel."

He looked at Cinder, scanning her face and body. She couldn't help but feel self-conscious that hair that had once hung in a clean, fragrant curtain around her body now hung in gnarled tangles. "Are you going to be all right for now if I leave you?" he asked.

Cinder nodded weakly, even though she wasn't sure that she would be.

Donte unraveled his arms from around her shoulders and walked to a group of his men. As one of Donte's men draped her in a light blanket, she glanced at the other women being assisted by some of the men. The only woman who wasn't crying or clinging to someone for comfort was Mistress Tula. Cinder saw her sitting there in her ragged clothing, burying her feet underneath the sand. She'd pick up fistfuls and let the grains of silica sift between the gaps of her fingers. Mistress Tula didn't look relieved as much as merely introspective about the whole situation. She was a woman of few words, but something seemed off.

Cinder crouched at her side. "Are you all right?" she asked.

"I'm not dead," Mistress Tula replied sharply. She pulled at her clothes, her superior dignity returning. "I'm not sure I know how to be afraid anymore."

In front of them, Donte and his militia readied their horses to leave. Mistress Tula only grabbed another handful of sand and eyed it as it streamed down her wrist.

Cinder found some tattered silks and wrapped one around her body. She could have gone and found the clothing that Nico had found for her, but the silk garment of one of the fallen women seemed more fitting now that she was part of the harem once again. "We're safe now," she tried to reassure the Mistress. She stood up and dusted off her knees. "Donte and his men will keep us safe. We can go back to the palace." Her words trailed off when she glanced over at Donte. Some of his men were herding the women and assisting them onto the horses.

"We are not safe. Your naïve optimism will get

you killed," she warned. "Do not think for a second that Jaden will let this end with today."

"Maybe they're scared of—"

Mistress Tula didn't even give her a chance to finish. "Cinder, everyone is scared." Giving a snort, she shook her head. "I guess I do know how to be afraid after all. We would all be fools not to be. But I assure you that Jaden is not through with us. They will return." She then finally trotted off to join the other women preparing to leave.

Cinder, overcome with fear once again, made her way toward Donte. She had to have faith. She had to believe that Donte and his men would keep her safe. She had to, or go mad with the darkest terror she ever knew. As she approached, Donte lifted her onto a horse and handed the reins to her.

"I'll be walking right beside you, so don't worry about how to ride," he said as he scanned the group, making sure all were secure and ready. He made eye contact with Cinder and gave a reassuring smile as he patted her leg. Then he gestured with a single wave. "Move out!"

17

The brutal sun baked the skin on their backs as they trekked through the utter ruins of a world squeezed dry. Cinder held her arm at her brow, bathed in sweat, shielding her face from the sun. She locked her eyes on Donte's flapping leather jacket, which was covered in streaks of dried blood. To her, he struck a gut feeling she couldn't quite put into words. Somehow, she just knew everything would be all right.

Donte led the crew, his gleaming sword dangling from his belt. In his hand, he twirled a dagger around between his fingers. Cinder's eyes narrowed in on the way his dark hair rested on his tanned neck. It curled slightly at the ends and shone brightly under the sun's rays. He had several days' worth of facial hair, which only added to his rugged, mysterious allure.

Ever since they'd started the journey, he walked beside her horse, but never said a word. She couldn't take the silence any longer.

"Are we heading back to the Palace of Lazar?"

Donte gurgled water in his mouth, then swallowed. "The palace was captured by Jaden." His words were like a punch to the gut. "We have another commune set up until we build up our forces and take the palace back."

"What about everyone else? The rest of the girls? Are they okay?" She was scared to ask the question. Scared of what the answer might be, but she had to know.

Donte placed the dagger he had been playing with back in its sheath. "Some are. Some lost their lives. We will know more when we all gather at Casen."

"Casen?"

"It's the commune we've been preparing for quite some time. It's always been our back up plan if something were to happen to the Palace of Lazar. It's in no way as nice as Lazar, but it will provide us with what we need for now." Donte's eyes gazed at the mottle of violet bruises covering her pale skin, making her self-conscious of her faded beauty. "We'll be able to provide medical care to those who need it as well as food, water and shelter."

A dry wind blew loose strands of her filthy hair. "Will Jaden come for us there?" Tears filled her eyes.

Donte drifted much closer to her side. "Eventually, I'm sure. But I promise you that if they do, we will be ready this time. Vengeance will be ours."

She gazed at the rough cracked skin on Donte's hands. "Are we at war? I remember hearing stories as a child... of great wars with no winners."

"There will be a winner in this one." His voice, so low and cool in tone, sent a shiver through her body.

"I'm scared." She couldn't hold back the tears any longer. Her cherished palace was gone and she was no more than a desert nomad, walking the wasted dunes, one day at a time.

Again.

Her fairytale no more.

Or did she ever truly have the fairytale?

Her dream had been shattered and now, with the thought of war, her nightmare of an existence had returned. She didn't want to live the life of her childhood again. Small, overcrowded communes infested with plague, hunger and hate—Briar was just one of many.

Donte's fingers curled tight on Cinder's fragile leg, and he looked up into her teary eyes when she flinched at his touch. "I'll make sure you are protected from this point on. I know you have been through a lot. More than I know, I'm sure, and more than I want to know. But I will never let you feel that fear again. Do you hear me?"

"You won't send us away like before?"

"No. Never again."

Cinder nodded, her lips slightly parted. No one had ever told her she mattered before. Even in Donte's cold roundabout way, he had made her feel special. She believed that he truly would try to keep her safe. Foolish maybe, to have such faith in someone, but what choice did she really have? Women of the communes didn't have many choices. She had learned that at a very early age.

Living at the palace gave her a life she'd never imagined. Silks, satins, jewels and luxury filled her days. Food and water were never a want, and comfort was never a need. The Palace of Lazar was her heaven. She cried harder at the thought of it all being gone.

Donte effortlessly hopped on the back of her horse without even having the horse stop. He wrapped his arms around her. "You'll be safe again. I'll make sure of it. Dry those tears," he soothed softly in her ear.

She nodded her head and sniffled back her tears to the best of her ability. His embrace gave her the strength she needed. "Thank you. I'm sorry for being such a burden. I know you need us all to be strong."

He stroked her matted hair. "You are strong, Cinder. You are much stronger than you know. There is no shame in being afraid." He tightened his grip around her. "Press back against me and rest."

She leaned back against his weight and wondered how much longer they'd travel before reaching Casen. Intense exhaustion throbbed deep in her lower back. By comparison, Donte didn't seem an ounce uncomfortable after marching beside the horse for nearly five hours.

Her lips parched, she felt sick to her stomach, battered and browbeaten by the sun. Drops of sweat ran down her arms. Her vision clouded and the ringing in her ears escalated, all the signs warning her that she was about to faint.

As if he, too, saw the warning signs, Donte put a flask of water to her lips. The cooling burn of water moistened her mouth. Cinder coughed into her fist.

"Donte," she rasped. "You don't need to waste your water on me."

"Shh... How are you feeling?"

"My throat... it's so tight."

He ever so gently held the back of Cinder's head. Her hair waterfalled through his big meaty fingers. "Drink up," he told her.

Cinder struggled to lift her arms and sip from Donte's flask. The lukewarm liquid shot down and stung her throat.

She stared up, relaxed in Donte's arms. Her hair swung in a tangled disarray, her clothes were in tatters, but she felt safe. Safely wrapped in Donte's embrace on a horse in a war-torn desert.

He looked at the sky, squinted up ahead, and then back at the sky again. "We'll need to stop and hole up here for a while. You'll have to bundle up. A sandstorm is coming."

"But what about Jaden? What if they catch up to us?"

"Jaden's army will not find us here. When I said I wouldn't let anyone hurt you, I meant it."

She breathed deeply, her small waifish body contorted in Donte's grasp. He dismounted from the horse, carrying Cinder through the crowd of soldiers and women. He gave the commands to his men, and his militia dropped their weapons and belongings, ready to set up a temporary shelter. They all saw to the rest of the women as if each girl had been assigned to them.

Dense layers of sand blew in the air. Looking out at the huddled masses, Cinder saw that each of them wore something wrapped around their faces. They hunkered down in the dead center of a sandstorm. Inhaling sand at this speed would scrape like gravel along the lining of your lungs, or suffocate you in your sleep. Blasting wind this high in the dunes would keep anyone—Jaden army or not—at bay. Cinder sat next to Donte, awaiting the storm.

"We'll return to Lazar," he said, and drew a picture in the sand with his dagger as they sat and waited for the storm to fully hit.

Cinder glanced down at the drawing of a palace with sun rays bouncing out of its borders. "The Palace of Lazar," she replied. "It was the only true home I knew."

Seconds later, the drawing vanished, blown away by the wind as the gusts picked up speed. The storm had reached them.

Donte pressed his body protectively against hers and wrapped his arm around her shoulder. "The storm will hopefully pass soon. Close your eyes and press your face against my chest."

She did as he ordered. The smell of leather from his clothing, and the essence of his body titillated her senses. The sand beat against her frame as Donte tried to pull her into him even closer. The noise of blowing wind conquered any sound. She couldn't even hear the horses that circled all the men and women, providing at least some minimal protection.

"Keep your eyes closed!" he yelled above the howling wind.

She tightened her eyes more and burrowed her face even deeper against his chest. The wind shook her body so hard that if it weren't for Donte holding her firm, she thought she might blow away. She remembered being told a story as a child of nomads being torn to shreds by the desert wind. The gory tale was told often to children to deter them from leaving to explore for something better. But sitting here, huddled against Donte, she couldn't help but wonder if the gruesome stories were indeed true.

He positioned his body so his covered lips were against her ear. "It's passing! Hold on just a little longer!" He rubbed her back reassuringly.

He held her like that until the worst of the storm had passed. When it finally subsided enough, he pulled away to examine her. "Are you all right?"

She removed the fabric from her face and nodded.

He stood up and surveyed the entire group. After seeing that everyone had weathered the storm, he gave his commands. "Let us continue on. Casen is near!"

18

The sun reflected off the sand, nearly blinding Cinder as she trekked across the desert. At one point, they stopped so he could wrap more cloth around their faces to prevent a sunburn from the scorching rays. Occasionally, a gust of wind blew sand into her face, and she was forced to travel forward with her eyes shut. The only protection she had from the sand blowing in her eyes was burying her face into Donte's frame. She clung to him for support, even though she hated having to. Every time she cuddled too close, the small sword in his satchel poked through the bag and nudged Cinder's leg, reminding her that at anytime they could be attacked by Jaden.

"Are we there yet?" she whispered. She didn't know if he heard her or not, but he didn't reply.

They traveled for a long time, and Cinder tried to estimate the minutes, but the heat was slowly sinking into her skin causing her head to pound. Her wounds started to sting and she felt her body fall limp against Donte.

The next thing she knew, she was on her back with Donte hovering over her. Her face was covered in liquid that didn't feel like sweat, and she realized that he had dumped the water from his flask over her face.

"You wasted all of that water on me." Guilt flooded her senses. He helped her sit up and she winced, gripping her side in pain. Everyone was staring at her with worry on their faces, and she hated the unwanted attention.

He helped her take a drink of water, scanning her body. "How are you feeling? Do you still feel faint?"

She shook her head, even though she wasn't sure she would be able to walk if she tried. The cloth he had tied to her head hours ago—hours or days ago—stuck to her head with dried sweat.

Donte sat down on the sand next to her, their shoulders touching. Cinder felt an added warmth come to her face and she tried to swallow, but her dehydration and the lump in her throat weren't helping.

After a short time, Donte helped her up to

stand. "We need to keep moving," he said with a new sense of urgency. He glanced around at everyone. "Drink water when needed, but we have to power on."

Cinder struggled to regain balance, blinking away her dizziness.

Donte wrapped his arm around her waist, pulling her next to his body for support. "Jaden's soldiers could be near. There's no telling where they are right now. We need to reach safety."

Cinder nodded and held on to his arm. He lifted her back onto the horse but the pain in her body was excruciating. Every bruise and every cut screamed against the heat of the sun.

"How long do you think it'll be until we find Casen?" she asked, feeling the sweat drip down her face.

"We'll reach Casen. I assure you."

She took a deep breath in through her mouth, but was greeted with sand filling every crack between her teeth. She grimaced at the gritty texture. She held her hand up to keep the dust from blowing into her eyes.

"We can do this," he said confidently. "With you by my side... we will succeed."

They rode until the sun finally reached the horizon, sinking. The moon made its appearance, and so did a cluster of stars.

"We'll stop here," Donte announced as he lowered her off the horse. Everyone else was doing the same around them.

Cinder didn't need him to say more. She let go of his arm and collapsed on the warm sand, thankful for a rest. They had traveled the rest of the day, gnawing on bits and pieces of food from Donte's satchel. In their food search of the commune before they left, they had found an extra flask of water, and they were able to steal the water from the fallen soldiers they had killed, which they took turns drinking.

She lay back on the sand, thankful it was cooling off. But she knew that soon the desert would turn into a frigid wasteland. Despite that, she let herself rest for a brief moment.

That moment turned into a few hours. They were awakened in the middle of the night by the sound of hissing. Donte bolted upright and held out his hands defensively. Cinder sat up just as quickly. At one point or another, she had crawled to Donte's side in the night to keep warm. She had been resting with her head on his chest. When he moved, it suddenly threw her to the sand.

"Shh," Donte commanded. He carefully stood up in one place and stuck his foot out to feel for the rock on which he'd placed his satchel.

The hissing intensified. Cinder drew her hands

to her chest. The hissing came from all directions and she didn't want to turn around, fearing what would be behind her.

Donte fumbled around in the darkness and found his satchel, drawing his small sword from it. He wielded the sword expertly. His hand remained steady as he glanced around in the complete blackness, no sign of fear in his expression.

The hissing sounded at his feet, and he instantly stabbed the sword down. The blade struck the sand with such an intensity that the ground shook, but he held the sword still. The blade sunk into the sand about halfway and he yanked it out.

The hissing ceased.

"Get up," he demanded of Cinder.

Cinder did as he ordered, cradling her side. The wound had opened up a little in her sleep and it stung under her hand. Pain shot up her leg and she gasped.

"Are you all right?" Donte whipped around to face her.

"What was that?" she asked, surprised to hear her own voice shaking a little.

Donte let out a long breath and dropped his arms to his sides. "A snake of some sort. I couldn't see if it was poisonous or not."

Cinder nodded and jumped when Donte reached for her hand.

"It's all right," Donte whispered as he grabbed her other hand. "It is just me. You're going to be fine. I killed the snake." He leaned in and placed a gentle kiss on her cheek. "We should wake everyone up and continue on while it's cool."

It didn't take long until the sun peeked over the horizon as they all rode toward Casen. She looked down at the man who chose to walk beside her. The faint light of morning colored Donte's face in pinks and yellows and oranges, and all of his sharp edges seemed softer. His usually piercing eyes were warmer, kinder.

"Is something wrong?" he asked, making eye contact with hers.

Cinder shook her head. "Nothing. I just feel safe being with you. Even now, I feel safe."

"We're far from safe," he mumbled as he undid the cloth from around his head and ran his hand through his hair. "But I promise you that I'll protect you. Snake or Jaden."

A gentle breeze fluttered through his hair, but nothing like the gusts of wind that had plagued them the day before. The flowing air was needed as they traveled on for miles and miles. Cinder was happy when they finally took a break from the grueling journey.

"How's your side?" he asked as they paused near a rare tree to give the horses water. Donte reached out to lift her silks.

"I'm fine, I think," she said. She sighed, though, and winced when he helped her sit down on the heated sand. Donte scowled as he gently pulled the silks off her side. The wound had opened again and was bleeding. The blood looked almost black in the dim light.

Donte removed the silks fully and instead replaced it with the cloth he'd been wearing around his head.

"Are you sure you want to do that?" Cinder said through gritted teeth. The pain hurt and she tried to not show it, but it stung just as much as it had the moment the attackers hurt her.

"Stay still," he ordered as he fastened the cloth around her side and then replaced the silks. "Not having a bandage could infect the wound. Not that this cloth is much better. We need to reach Casen and attend to this immediately."

Cinder remained silent. She sat back and looked down at her hands, rough and worn from wear and tear. She had a few calluses on her palms and fingers, and her nails were broken off.

The moment of silence expanded between them. She could hear chatter from the other soldiers and harem girls, but it all was just a murmur of sound. Cinder glanced up to see the sun rising gradually above the horizon, painting the sky in an array of colors. It looked almost like a watercolor painting, all the colors blended together with no telling of where one color ended and the next began.

"It's lovely," she murmured. It had been a long time since she had seen anything of beauty and was happy that she was still able to take a moment and appreciate what still remained good in life. She absently drew circles in the sand with the tip of her finger.

"I'm gazing at something much prettier," Donte said quietly.

Cinder froze, her heart skipping a beat. Donte stood up and walked to his satchel. When she turned to look at him, she found him wiping his sword, which was still stained with the blood of the snake he had killed in the darkness.

Cinder shook her head and carefully got to her feet.

"What do you think you're doing?" He tucked the blade in his satchel and hurried to her, wrapping his arms around her torso.

"I feel better," she said. "We need to keep moving." Cinder didn't want her weakness to be the reason for their failure. She needed to find her strength.

"Are you sure your side is free from pain?"

Cinder paused to look at him. His angled face was covered in worry and concern.

She nodded with a weak smile. "Ride with me."

After a few minutes of riding, she rested her head against his shoulder, allowing his strength to help carry her on.

The sun rose higher and higher, and Cinder used this to gauge what time it was. As soon as it stood overhead, she knew it was around noon.

They proceeded to walk as the sun moved across the sky. The gusts of wind grew stronger, throwing Donte and Cinder back and forth. Sand littered the sky, as well as other little bits of debris. When the wind became too strong, Donte pulled Cinder closer to keep her from falling off the horse.

Several hours later, night fell and Cinder didn't hesitate to completely collapse.

"Are you all right?" Donte asked, swooping to her side.

"Just tired," she said through a vicious yawn. "The heat really takes a lot out of you."

Donte sat down beside her. "You should have told me if you needed to rest."

In the near-darkness, the desert didn't look so threatening. The darkness brought a light breeze, not biting gusts of wind, and cooler temperatures, not scorching ones. Cinder dug her hand into the sand and found cooler grains below the surface.

Donte rummaged through his satchel. "Here, eat." When she paused and looked at the rest of the harem girls settling in, he added, "Don't worry. Each soldier has been assigned to care for them. They'll eat too."

She took a scrap of dried fruit from him. He pulled out his near-empty flask. He took a small sip before handing it to Cinder.

Donte breathed in deeply before letting it out in a heavy breath. "We better find Casen soon."

"I know," she murmured. She pulled herself to Donte's side. "Can we start a fire? It's getting cold."

"No," he said flatly. "As much as I want to, we cannot. We can't risk showcasing our location to whatever else is in this desert. Jaden is looking for us right now, and we can't draw them a map to where we are by building a fire."

Cinder nodded and buried her face in his shoulder. "But we won't get attacked by snakes tonight, will we?"

He chuckled, a noise she hadn't heard in a long time. Laughter. "I hope not."

"If we do, you'll save us again," she said. "Hopefully."

"Hopefully?" Donte repeated with a chuckle.

"I'll risk my life for you, Cinder. Now get some sleep."

"Maybe we should continue on," Cinder protested, but a yawn escaped her lips. Despite her protests, she fell into a deep sleep against Donte.

The sound of clopping suddenly made her sit up. Two horses appeared in the distance and Donte quickly got to his feet. He scrambled for his satchel and dug out his small sword, wielding it in front of him.

When Cinder saw the sword, she gasped and turned to look where he was looking. There were two Jaden warriors.

She ran to her own satchel and pulled out another small blade, raising it and letting the faint light gleam against it.

"I'm ready to fight," she said as she pulled herself to Donte's side.

Before he could protest, more warriors approached them, weapons hanging from their belts. Without a word, one of them charged toward them, wielding a lengthy sword. All the men jumped up from their slumber prepared for battle with sleepy eyes.

As one Jaden soldier charged, Donte matched it, and the sounds of the cries of the harem and blades colliding rang through the air. Cinder jumped out of the way, only to see a Jaden warrior running at her. Her small blade didn't compare to his sword and she wished that Donte had better weapons for the harem and not just his men.

For now, all she could do was duck and avoid being stabbed. The soldier grabbed her and shoved her to the ground, knocking her small dagger out of her hand. The man pinned her to the sand, and reached for her fallen blade.

Then, Donte shoved the warrior out of the way, shoving his own blade into the warrior's neck. Cinder grimaced and turned away, only to see the first warrior rising from the ground and bolting in their direction. She rolled out of the way just as he swiped his sword at Donte.

She scrambled to her feet as Donte engaged the first in a battle of colliding blades. She stood there helpless, not sure how she could help Donte fight the remaining soldier. She closed her eyes in panic, wishing for the violence to go away. The sound of metal striking metal pierced her ears, followed by a grunt from a man.

When she opened her eyes, she saw the warrior on the ground, bleeding from a gash on the throat. Donte stood where the warrior had been moments before, his blade bloody. He was breathing heavily, scanning the two bodies that bled on the sand. He ran off to assist his men in killing the rest of Jaden, which fortunately they did successfully.

They had won another victory. Small, but still a victory.

"Did they hurt you?" Donte asked, scooping her up into his arms.

She shook her head faintly.

He held her for a moment, rocking her back and forth, kissing her on her head repeatedly. She could feel his heartbeat against his chest, his breath ragged.

When his breathing steadied, he gestured to the horses. "We need to get moving and find Casen before more Jaden soldiers come."

Cinder nodded and slipped her hand into his, heading for the horses. Donte helped her up onto her horse, and he pulled himself onto one of Jaden's as his men did the same with the extra horses gained in their night battle. He fiddled with the pockets of the makeshift saddles, eventually finding small pouches of food.

"Open the pockets of the saddle," he said eagerly to his men. "There may be food, water, and a few weapons, as there is in mine."

The men did as he said and pulled out a few bags of dried fruit, just like what Donte had. They searched a bit more and found a few small knives, as well as canisters of clean water.

Before she could stop herself, Cinder moved her horse to where Donte was, grabbed his extended water canister and drank, letting the cool water hydrate her dry, cracked mouth and lips.

After, she turned to see Donte doing the same thing. They both grinned and shared a bag of dried fruit, knowing there was much more in the saddle pockets.

"We will definitely be able to cover some ground with these extra horses that are clearly rested and fed, and now our supplies have been replenished," Donte said cheerfully.

Cinder stroked her hand down the mane of her horse. She had never ridden before without Donte at the very least walking beside her, but she was confident she would manage.

As the sun started to peek over the horizon, they rode off.

Everyone rode quietly through the day, finding it a lot quicker than some of them walking. With the horses they were able to cover at least three times the distance than they had before.

Finally, they came to a stop when the sun started to set and let the horses rest. Cinder, despite not having to do anything physical, felt worn out and exhausted. Even Donte offered a yawn as he slid off his horse.

"I feel like we're not going to be able to find Casen," Cinder muttered as she rummaged through the pockets on the saddle. "We're going to run out of supplies sooner or later."

Donte nodded. "We will reach it. And with the horses, we'll be able to reach it quicker. Everything will be fine. Don't lose faith."

Cinder shrugged her shoulders tiredly and sat down on the sand. "I hope so. If we don't find it soon, I'm afraid we'll die." She hated to say the words, but couldn't resist doing so. Her spirits were as beaten as her body.

"We'll reach it," Donte repeated stonily. He sat down next to her and held out his arms.

Cinder smiled a little to herself as she snuggled against his broad chest and watched the desert fade before her eyes as the sun sank below the horizon. Soon, she was no longer able to see anything, even things inches from her face.

She heard the horses breathe heavily as they settled down for rest, and the wind rustling sand back and forth. No snakes, no warrior attacks. Just pure darkness.

THE LIGHT of early morning woke Cinder, and she found herself cuddled closely to Donte, her head resting on his chest. His arm was around her, holding her close to him.

Without waking him, she sat up and rubbed her eyes. The horses were still there where they had left them. Nothing had changed about the desert.

Donte yawned and opened his eyes sleepily. "Good morning," he said as he scanned the surroundings and horses. He rose and made his way over to his horse. He pulled a canister of water from one of the saddle pouches and poured water into the palm of his hand. His horse greedily lapped it up. Cinder watched him and did the same. They both took a sip from the canister to wet their mouth and throat, then put it back in the saddle pouch. Everyone else was stirring and preparing for another long day of trekking the desert toward their new commune.

"Let us keep moving. We should be there soon," he called out loudly as he helped Cinder mount.

She watched him slide gracefully onto the back of his horse and before she knew it, they were riding again.

Just like every day they had spent in the desert so far, the sun was hot and grueling, and the sand blew like a vortex around them. At one point, Cinder leaned forward and pressed her face into the horse's mane.

The heat exhausted her to the point where Cinder almost started seeing things. She had a constant headache and the scenery changed colors before her eyes. Instead of golden sand, it changed to red sand, crimson like the color of blood. At one point during the day, she thought she saw a cluster of palm trees and nearly fell off her horse trying to get to them. Donte had to splash her with water to knock her out of the delusion.

They needed to find Casen, and soon.

As the hours passed, the heat seemed to intensify and the horses grew weaker with each step. Clothes stuck to everyone's bodies due to the amount of sweat they produced. Cinder wanted to talk as they traveled, but her mouth was unbearably dry and she could barely articulate her words.

Finally, the sun hit two or three in the afternoon and Cinder could hardly see straight. She glanced to the side to see Donte staring at her with concern. He moved to pull a canister of water from the saddle and handed it to her.

"Drink, Cinder. Stay with me." His voice was raspy, a sign that the desert took a toll on him as well. He pointed off in to the distance. "Look, Cinder. Casen."

Cinder narrowed her eyes and lifted her head, looking where he was pointing. Then, she saw trees.

"Are those actual trees?" she asked anxiously.

"Am I really seeing trees and not just hallucinating?"

Donte kicked his horse, galloping off. Cinder kicked her horse and followed closely behind as did everyone else. She could see by the facial expressions of her fellow harem ladies, that they were as stunned as she was.

It didn't take long to close the distance, but soon they stood in front of a large building surrounded by luscious trees.

"Welcome to Casen," Donte said as he helped her off the horse. He gestured toward the large structure. "This is the housing unit for all the soldiers, but we'll stop here to rest and drink. I'll then show you our new home."

Cinder felt heat rush to her face, and then Donte's arms were around her. She felt his hands thread through her sweaty hair and she leaned against him, her face pressing into the curve of his neck.

"Can you stand?" he asked, clearly concerned.

She nodded. "I'm fine. Everything is now fine." She looked up into his eyes and stared for a long moment, feeling as if she could see his soul, the connection between them unbreakable.

She pulled back to look at him, but before she could say another word, he dipped forward to press his lips hotly to hers. Their bodies molded together flawlessly as she kissed him back, her lips exploring his mouth with tenderness rather than hunger. His hands touched every part of her body that they could, and the heat between them intensified.

A kiss of celebration.

A kiss of hope.

19

Glimmers of the rising sun spread its warmth over the flat horizon. The commune of Casen lay just up ahead. Cinder looked at the very crude structure; a far cry from the Palace of Lazar. A circular wall was in the process of being built by men, and watch towers were also being constructed. Barbed wire coiled along the top of wooden pylons, sharpened at their tips. Clearly, this commune was preparing for an attack. It didn't look like any paradise, but it would have to be their new home.

"Help the women, and get the horses to the stables," Donte commanded his men. "Rest up for the evening. You did a good job out there. We're lucky to have you on our side." His praise to them seemed welcome as each man approached Donte with a pat on the back or a shake of the hand before heading off.

The women of the harem stood with only Donte in the entrance of the heavily guarded commune.

"They call this a commune," Mistress Tula murmured under her breath. Cinder turned to her in the harsh desert sunlight.

"Does anything satisfy you, really?" Cinder asked, annoyed by the woman's attitude. She knew there had been a time she was to respect and follow every command this woman gave. But things had changed, and Cinder grew to detest this woman. Mistress Tula was supposed to be their leader. She was expected to escort the harem to safety. And although it wasn't her fault they were captured, just as it wasn't Cinder's fault her group had also been taken, Mistress Tula was far from a leader. She didn't offer anything to the situation that any of the other girls didn't. She didn't offer guidance, comfort or strength. The only thing she had done during the entire journey was bitch and complain. And when they faced rape and death with Jaden, she'd cowered behind them all.

"Why are you so easily satisfied?" Mistress Tula calmly shot back. "I know you think we are now safe in this place, but this is not what I would consider an appropriate shelter. Jaden could crush us in seconds here."

Cinder shrugged her shoulders and walked away. Maybe she was crazy, but as she watched Donte talking to some other men in his small army, she felt safe.

"They've arrived! They're here!" Elbi called out.

Elbi came walking out of a large building, with pure joy on her face. Cinder's heart stopped at the sight of her. *Elbi!* She was alive! Her group of women must have arrived safely.

Elbi looked at the swath of filthy, clearly exhausted women with a huge smile on her face. Her eyes made contact with Cinder's and she came running toward her.

"Cinder!" she cried, as she wrapped her arms around her. She pulled away and examined Cinder's body. "Are you all right? Are you hurt anywhere?"

Cinder shook her head as tears cascaded down her face.

"I'm so happy to see you. I was so scared you were all killed." Elbi pulled away and hugged and greeted the rest of the women, scanning their bodies for injuries as well.

"Where did you find them?" Mistress Krin

asked as she approached the harem from the doors of Casen as well. You could tell she was just as pleased as Elbi was.

Donte unloaded his horse as he spoke. "We rescued them from some Jaden soldiers. General Rhys was there."

"Did you kill him?" Mistress Krin asked, with contempt in her voice.

Donte shook his head. "The bastard ran, but not before killing some of our men and slitting the throats of two of our women." He turned to Elbi and then Mistress Krin. "Do you mind getting the women cleaned, fed and cared for? They've been though quite an ordeal."

Elbi and Mistress Krin both nodded silently and motioned for all the women to follow them. Cinder didn't want to leave Donte. She loved Elbi, but her paralyzing fear returned at the thought of not having him there to protect her.

"Cinder," Donte gestured Cinder over. He clearly could read the fear written across her face.

When he called her name, her small heart beat faster, booming in her chest. She quickly stood before him.

"You're going to be all right now. Go and get cleaned up with Elbi and Mistress Krin. I promise that you're safe."

He looked at Mistress Krin again. "Show the women to their new home. Some of them need medical care and wounds cleaned."

Elbi grabbed Cinder's hand and led her away from Donte and the other soldiers.

Cinder took a deep breath to calm the panic clutching her heart. She tugged at her scraps of clothing, realizing she needed to do as Donte ordered.

"Does this place keep them out? The Jaden army, I mean?" Her voice shook, almost as badly as her body.

Elbi squeezed her hand reassuringly. "They haven't found us yet. This commune is really in the depths of the dunes. Plus, allied forces are arriving daily. Soon we will be strong enough to fight them. Don't worry." Elbi looked over her shoulder at the rest of the harem following them. "We are all safe for now."

Cinder desperately wanted that to be true.

SHE TOSSED and turned in bed, trying to sleep as Donte directed once the harem was cleaned and fed. The hushed voices of Donte and several men behind the door pulled her attention. She wanted to be with them. Being in this foreign room, with just the harem, reminded her of all the pain she had endured since leaving the harem.

Nothing would be the same again.

Her mind brought her to the brink of madness, and she had to distract her thoughts. She got out of bed and padded her way to the main room of Casen, hoping Donte wouldn't mind. She paused in the hallway to hear what they were saying.

"More allies are coming," one of the commanders said.

"Have our men found all the women of the harem?" Donte's voice sounded tired as he asked the question.

"All the surviving ones."

"What about this man Cinder speaks of? Have you found his body based on her description?" Donte asked. "Nico?"

"There have been a lot of men killed recently. It's just too hard to know if any of them are this man who offered assistance."

"The allies need to arrive soon. Jaden is stronger now. With the fall of Lazar, they now have our resources, our horses... everything that once belonged to us," Donte said.

"We'll get it all back or die trying. We'll regroup and conquer." The commander who spoke sounded confident, and Cinder couldn't help but be grateful for the positive outlook in such a dark time.

"No one knows if the prince survived the attack or not," a soldier said. "The lack of this knowledge helps keep you safe."

"I don't care if they know if I'm alive or not," Donte said. "They should fear the prince of Lazar. Not the other way around."

Prince of Lazar?

Cinder stepped into the room. "Prince?" she asked confused. "Donte, did I hear you correctly?"

Donte and the soldiers turned in her direction the minute she entered.

"What are you doing out of bed? You were told to rest," Donte said with anger tinting his voice.

"I can't sleep. And besides, I'm fine." She took a few steps further into the room. "What were you discussing?"

Donte glanced at one of the commanders who nodded.

He took a few steps to her and placed his hand on her lower back. "Back to bed."

Cinder shrugged away from his touch. "What did they mean when they said *prince*?"

Donte took a deep breath. "I'm the prince of Lazar. I'm the man who *once* reigned over Lazar."

She looked at the soldiers who tried to appear as if they weren't listening to the conversation and then back at Donte. "I don't understand. Why the secrecy? Why would you not admit to being the prince to me?" Her voice faded off at the last part of the question.

"Because I enjoyed observing. I enjoy overseeing the training of the harem. I can see truth in each of the women, see their true intentions."

"But we were being trained for... for you. Why wouldn't you just make it known you are the prince from the beginning?"

"Keeping my identity private when someone first joins the palace was a decision I made when I built it. I have also never revealed my identity to anyone outside of the palace. I wanted to build the allure, the mystery, but not actually be removed from the daily activity. The unknown created myths and stories. It was a way to see the loyalty of the harem and all involved before they learned the truth. Protecting my identity helped protect the palace. In a merciless world, I guarded myself from assassinations by concealing who I was. And right now, my secrecy has worked to my advantage. Jaden has no idea if I'm alive or dead. They have no idea I'm planning a counterattack," Donte added.

The commander nodded. "No one, other than a

few members of the harem, knows what the prince looks like."

Cinder nodded in understanding. Her mind blurred with the onslaught of information.

Wait... did she understand?

She couldn't help but feel lied to. Fooled. She had sex with the prince all along. She was obsessing, and forming intense feelings for... the prince! It never crossed her mind that Donte was the prince. Even Elbi and the other harem girls never let on that Donte was the prince. Although they had never denied the fact or even acted like Donte was anything but. They had said no one speaks of their time with the prince, but...

Donte placed his hand in the familiar spot on her back. "That is enough for now," he said in a low voice.

Cinder looked up into his stern, but concerned, eyes.

"We have a lot to do tomorrow, and you need to regain as much strength as possible."

"I've trekked through the desert many times, Donte. I can rebound fast." Defiance was not becoming of a harem girl, but she was salty about this new knowledge.

Did it change anything that Donte was the prince?

No, not really. But regardless, she was salty.

"Cinder, this is not a conversation I'm going to have. Leave us now, and go back to bed."

She shook her head. "I'm fine." She limped toward a nearby chair and almost sat down when she heard his voice, freezing her in her tracks.

"Cinder, to the room, now!" He pointed to a door leading to a room she had yet to be in.

"But..." She considered pushing him even further, but wisdom won over.

"This instant."

She looked at the soldiers as if they were going to step in and plead her case. They stood or sat with their arms across their chests with the same firm expression as Donte. Realizing she wasn't going to win this battle, she turned and quickly made her way to the room—Donte following close behind.

It was a private sleeping quarters, and she assumed it was Donte's... *Prince* Donte.

She sat on the bed and looked up at him. "I'm sorry, I should have stayed in bed," Cinder said quietly. "I didn't mean to disobey you, but I just can't lie there and not have my mind race."

"You need your rest. What's still ahead of us is going to take all your strength."

Cinder studied her palms and nodded.

"How's the wound on your side?" he asked.

"It's wrapped. I really am not injured as badly as it appears."

Donte nodded his approval. "Good."

"I'm stronger than you think."

Donte nodded again. "Have you lost your submission? Has your strength suffocated the surrender you once had?" he asked quietly.

"I'm afraid I'm not the harem girl anymore. Maybe I never was. I wanted to be, but when faced with the reality of our world... I have to be a fighter. A survivor. I have to be ruthless and even selfish to stay alive. I pictured myself when I finally found the palace as it being a perfect utopia. Ball gowns, extravagant parties, caviar and champagne, beautiful dancing women, and a prince who would find me the most beautiful of them all and choose me. But all my visions shattered. Like glass. Into a million shards. I'm afraid I am not that fairytale princess I had so hoped to be. I can't be."

Donte studied her. "No, indeed you are not. But I need to show you that there is power in compliance. It takes more strength to submit."

"How will you show me that?" Cinder asked, pulling her knees up to her chest, hugging them tightly.

Donte's stern blue eyes found hers. "I think you know the answer to your question."

Cinder nodded, as Donte sat at the edge of the bed and patted his leg.

She understood the sensual invitation and removed her clothing without having to be asked. Letting her clothes pool at her feet, she laid her nude body over his lap in silence.

"I'm ready to submit to your discipline." Was she? Even though she said the words, she didn't know if she truly was ready. Had that part of her, even with all the training, died?

Cinder clutched the sheets of the bed and closed her eyes. Taking a deep breath, she relaxed her body over his muscled thighs. She *had* missed the sensation of giving herself to Donte and his firm control.

The sound of the first spank echoed in the sparsely furnished room. Her surprised gasp followed. Keeping quiet for the sake of the soldiers would most likely be futile. No doubt the men in the next room would know that Donte was spanking her bare behind. Shame fueled by the sting of the continuous spanking sent her emotions spiraling. Tears threatened to fall, but for some reason, she couldn't let them release. A wall blocked the flow.

After a few more slaps to naked flesh, Donte paused and rubbed her heated skin. His hand parted her legs and found the wetness the correction caused. He rubbed his finger along her silky folds, collecting the signs of her arousal. With a slick finger, he pressed against her anus until the puckered flesh opened. He drove his finger past her asshole and let it rest in her depths.

"I know you have had to be a fighter, Cinder. I know you have had no choice but to allow dominance to take over that purity inside of you. I am so proud of you for being able to do so. But I don't want you to lose that softness I have grown so fond of."

As he pumped his finger in and out, Cinder allowed the wall to crumble. A deep wave of erotic submission took over. She belonged to him. Donte gave her the gift of surrender back. The tightness left her body. The tension disappeared, and she once again felt like the safe, secure harem girl she thought she had lost in the desert.

He continued to spank with his free hand at the same rhythm of the thrusting finger. In and out, spank after spank, Donte demanded she give her body and soul to him. All the ugly, all the death, everything that threatened to eat her alive seemed so far away at the moment. Her mind drifted to a place of refuge.

Her body hummed by the time the spanking ended. She didn't fight this one. She didn't beg for him to stop. Although the spanking hurt, it wasn't what she would consider a punishment. She needed it. Her body craved it. Her soul required it to heal. Donte spanked, allowing her to feel an emotion she thought she would never feel again... safe.

Her world was spinning hard upon the axis of desire. She wanted him more than anything. "Take me, Donte. I've never needed anything more. I need you more than I needed water crossing the desert to get here."

He pulled her off his lap and pressed her wanting body against the bed. In fluid motions, he removed his clothing before her eyes. "I only take what is mine."

She licked her lips in anticipation and spread her legs, beckoning. "I am yours. I have always been yours."

His eyes darkened. "Yes, that's true. And not just because I'm the prince. But simply because you are. You are mine and will remain mine always."

He lowered his nude body on top of hers and pressed his mouth firmly to her moistened lips. Claiming her mouth, sending warning bells of what he would be claiming next, he moaned against her gasp.

He growled as he spread her thighs wider with his legs.

His hand that had just delivered pain, now lowered to her pussy to deliver pleasure.

"Donte..." she breathed, her eyes closing as she pushed her hips to meet his thrusting finger. Her juices coated his hand as he readied her.

He pressed his cock at the opening and whispered, "I want you to relax. This may still hurt like before. I'm not a small man, and this hole of yours is tight." He placed kisses all over her neck with great tenderness.

Cinder tried to do as he said, but as he slowly entered her, the pressure built until a wave of intense sensation erupted inside her. She cried out as he pressed all the way in. He paused and kissed her deeply, not moving, allowing her pussy to accept his girth. He pulled away enough so their gazes met and united just as their bodies did.

"Slow, we are going to take this very slow," he whispered hoarsely.

He began to thrust in and out of her in graceful, sensual movements. Every move left her breathless, giving her a pleasure almost too much to bear.

His lips caressed the skin of her face as he murmured, "No person has possessed my heart as you do, my sweet Cinder."

To feel his body take her so completely took her to a level of joy that brought tears to her eyes.

His tender movements moved in and out in such a slow dance of seduction she didn't realize the crescendo of ecstasy was sneaking up on her. Without warning, her body exploded around his plunging cock as she screamed out his name.

"I am yours," she screamed against his chest. "I am yours!"

20

The morning sun dipped behind the clouds, chilling the air with its shadow. Cinder sat on a wooden bench on the back side of the main structure with a blanket wrapped tightly around her shoulders. A gentle breeze blew her hair into her face. Blackbirds cawed in the sky—their fragile wings carrying them through the air above the palms with ease. The yard was quiet, peaceful, and serene. It reminded Cinder of the palace. A life she wasn't sure she would ever live again.

She missed the life of the harem, and everything she had experienced at the palace. She couldn't help but feel that a chapter in all their lives was over, never to be read again. She worried for all of them. Worried that the rest of the harem would not survive an attack by Jaden. The unknown haunted her.

The closing of the door behind her shoulder broke the silence. "It's time we teach you how to fight." Donte pulled a bow from behind his back, his devious, coy smile making her nervous. "Are you ready to learn how to shoot it?"

The hair on her arms stood, and her stomach churned with the thought of holding a weapon in her hands, let alone shooting it. Weapons and violence were against everything she believed in. She was a fighter, but not a killer... at least not by choice. But she supposed she actually was a killer now after she had killed her attacker brutally.

Why did she need to learn even more ways to kill? She knew she was foolish by even questioning. The war had just begun.

"Why? Do you think Jaden will come here next?"

"We are safe for now. But that doesn't mean you don't need to learn how to defend yourself."

The thought of killing another person nearly made her want to vomit. Her most recent kill would haunt her for the rest of her life.

"Do you see those trees over there?" he said, pointing north from where they stood. Ten or twenty yards away, two small palms were spread a few feet apart from one another.

"So do you truly do believe there will be a war? One where I'll be expected to fight?" she asked.

He ignored her first question and handed her the bow. "Everyone should know how to shoot an arrow, Cinder. Never depend on someone else for your survival. Never."

He truly had no idea what she had been through, but she wasn't exactly going to share the details. She feared her fragile mind could break again.

He began explaining his technique, his fingers gliding over the wood, string, and arrowhead, pointing at different parts as he described their function and demonstrated how to stand and release. He slipped a bracer on her left arm and tightened it, then assisted her into a leather breastplate as well.

"This is just to protect your delicate skin from the sting of the bowstring," he cautioned her.

Next, he stood behind her, his hands on her hips as he guided her into position at right angles to the target trees. He nocked an arrow just below the bead, and helped her to draw the bowstring back fully to the anchor point. His arms were around her, distracting her. His breath was warm on her neck.

"Relax. Archery has more in common with art than war. It's a dance between you, your target, and the tools in your hands. Feel the breeze in your hair. Where's it coming from? How will it affect the arrow's flight path? Breathe in, breathe out. Hold your back straight, keep your posture tall, proud, as if you had a crown on your head."

His words floated around her, embracing her. Under his guidance, she sighted the arrow and relaxed her fingers. The string snapped, striking her breastplate and bracer, and she was suddenly grateful for the protective coverings Donte had given her. The arrow flew with only a slight waver, striking the closer tree near its base.

"Again," Donte said. He stepped back, guiding her to nock the next arrow on her own. His face beamed with pride.

She released five more arrows before Donte led her out to view the targets. Different colored feathered arrows stuck out from the target.

"You have great aim, Cinder. You're a natural as I had no doubt you would be. You'll always be my perfect fighter, my warrior," he said.

She liked pleasing him. "Thank you. But you need to tell me the real reason for this lesson."

Donte smiled. "I can't get anything by you." His expression grew serious. "The last of our allied forces is coming."

"You say that as if that's a bad thing." Cinder grew anxious.

"You knew this day would come." Worry blanketed his face. "They're marching through the desert to relocate here. Then, as you asked, we will prepare for war. For complete annihilation of Jaden." He reached for her hands and held them to his chest. "I don't want to get your hopes up, but I also have reason to believe that Nico is alive."

Her loud gasp came simultaneously with her tears. "What? He is? Oh my God!"

Donte swiped at her tears she didn't even know were falling. "We believe so. He's injured a bit, but my men are bringing him here." He kissed her tear-stained cheek. "We'll know for certain when they arrive. If indeed this man is Nico, I'll forever be in his debt for saving you."

Cinder released the breath she had been holding. "But? I see there's more in the way you look."

"It is time we get ready, Cinder. It is time we conquer Lazar and make the palace ours once again."

"We?"

He nodded. "Yes, *we*. I'll never send you away again. I need my fighter standing by my side."

───────────

CINDER WATCHED the faces of the other harem

women as Donte spoke to the higher ranking commanders in hushed tones of the war's developments and as, with intense remorse, they named all who had died, breaking her heart even more. Fear, anger, denial—she saw all of it written large on their faces. Donte did not seem to see it on them, for he only looked at her as he explained what would come next: they were to prepare for battle. All that the prince had built and worked for was in the hands of Jaden; who came to ransack the palace and claim it as their own. These beasts were now in her gardens where she loved to tend to her flowers and walk peacefully, listening to the call of a peacock or a coo of a dove. Her paradise was no more.

Cinder cleared her throat and unfurled one of her shapely legs from beneath her, savoring the cool kiss of the room's tile on her skin. She thought of how much she missed the warmth of the ornate rugs she sat on at the palace as she spoke. "Are we safe? Will Jaden come and attack Casen like they did Lazar?"

She watched Donte's face contort with the pain of telling a hard truth. He finally looked away from her and took in the expressions of the other women.

He inhaled deeply before answering Cinder's question. "You will all be guarded thoroughly. My men and I will not let any harm come to any of you again. We have soldiers to guard you around the clock. All of you. They are among our best, and are the strongest men we could find. They'll let no harm befall you," he said.

"And what if we are taken anyway? What if by some strange fate one or all of us is left unattended and we're stolen? It will mean certain death, you know this!" Cinder did not mean to be insolent but it was her fear that spoke through her. Gruesome thoughts of Maysa's death washed over her.

"That's what I wanted to tell you all. For the next few weeks, we'll dedicate as much time as possible to teaching you how to defend yourselves. You'll learn how to fight," Donte declared, clearly hating the words himself.

Elbi gasped and asked, "You want us *all* to fight? To *kill*?" Her voice was high-pitched and shrill, like that of a terrified girl.

Cinder watched as Donte looked at Elbi, his eyes pleading that she, that all of them, understand. "Only if you must. I can't bear the thought of you being at the whim of a Jaden soldier." His eyes now scanned the faces of all of the women and finally came to rest back upon Cinder.

"Do you know when Jaden will be here?" Cinder asked.

The other women watched them speak, their eyes flitting from Donte to Cinder and back. Cinder had earned their respect and though she was typically quite timid in her speech, especially to Donte, she spoke now with a fervor and a fear they all felt.

"We sent men to spy at the dunes and see if they were close. As of last night, they couldn't be found. Our other men are skimming the desert, looking for them. We believe that they are still a few weeks away. Even on the fastest horse, the journey here is long. And we are hidden well," Donte answered.

"What about the training of the harem?" Mistress Lana piped up. "If they are busy learning to fight, when shall we have time to train them in their duties as a harem girl? If we teach them dominance, how are we to teach them submission at the same time?"

The women began to whisper all around, and Donte did nothing to silence their mild clucking.

"The harem must change. Survival is what we must focus on or the harem will no longer exist. The best way we can protect all of you is by teaching you how to protect yourselves." He took a deep breath and looked around at the commanders who nodded in agreement. "If something were to happen to us, we don't want to leave you all helpless," Donte added. "We assure you, we'll do everything we can within our power to restore the harem as it once was. But for now, I ask you to respect my men. I also expect to you to respect me. Not as the prince who ruled the Palace of Lazar, but as the general of this new army," Donte said with a renewed sense of authority.

Despite the fact Cinder was uncomfortable with the idea of learning how to fight, after learning the art of submission and seduction, she saw Donte hurting with all the upheaval, and her heart opened to him. "You'll always have our respect. And if you say to us now that you believe this will protect us, then that is what we'll do of course," Cinder said, her voice barely above a whisper.

Mistress Krin leaned forward and rose to her feet, gracefully. She brushed some of the dust from her silk robes. "The training begins tomorrow morning?" she asked.

The other mistresses began to rise, following her lead.

Without hesitation, Donte replied, "Before dawn."

The mistresses motioned for all the women of the harem to follow them and began to file out but Cinder stayed, looking at Donte for a moment hoping he would ask her to remain. She didn't want to leave his side ever again, and hoped he felt the same way.

"You'll be safe with the other women, Cinder," he reassured her.

"Of course. Good night, sir," she said as she hurriedly left, the echoes of her footfalls reverberating through the empty halls. His words hurt, but she struggled to push them aside. He had a war to fight, and she had to be patient and understanding that his focus had to be directed elsewhere. Although with the memories of the night before still lingering, she couldn't help but feel greedy and want more.

21

Cinder awoke to the sound of men beneath her window, talking quietly. Their voices were far away at first but as the sleep left her body and the fog cleared from her mind, she could hear a heated discussion. She heard Donte, whose voice she knew, as well as a commander, and then another one. As she tried to discern what they were discussing from afar, she watched the moonlight dapple the walls of her chamber. The sky was still dark, and morning was a few hours away yet. She heard the locusts chirping in the wasteland, mixed with the heavy breathing of the women of the harem. They were all scattered about on makeshift beds in an empty, cold room. She stood and wrapped her half naked body in a heavier piece of muslin. Cinder tiptoed toward the window and leaned against the edge. She did not want to be seen, but she eavesdropped anyway. When she closed her eyes to concentrate on the third voice, she could hear him more clearly.

"You informed me that we'll be training the harem tomorrow. To be honest, Donte, I don't know if they'll ever be able to learn what we can teach them. Especially in such a short period of time, and if we are forced to leave here earlier than planned..." the man spoke with a quiet urgency.

"I understand your concerns, Nico, but you'll do with this time whatever you can to make these women strong. If the Jaden army somehow manages to take them, the only hope they have of survival is going to be whatever ferocity they can manage in the first few minutes of their capture. Even if they do escape, they'll need the fortitude to make it through the swaths of the desert for any amount of time and then find their way back to us," Donte said.

Nico! Nico! It was him. Cinder had no doubt by the sound of his voice. Nico had survived the attack!

"These women have never even known the outside world... or at least not in a very, very long time. They've never gone a day without food in ages, or at least since joining the Palace of Lazar. They avoid the hot sun by bathing in the pools of

Lazar's garden or lounging under the palms. If they're captured, death might be a better fate for them than traveling through the desert alone with no water, no food, and probably not even some idea of what direction they should be going." Nico said this with more urgency, and Cinder shuddered at the thought of what the man was implying. In her mind, it did not really seem that far-fetched; the fate he was describing.

"I'm forever in your debt, Nico. You saved Cinder's life and almost lost your own in doing so. I'm asking if you'll help us train them. If you say no, I'll respect that. But don't question my decision that I made with some of the best commanders and soldiers in what's left of this world," Donte warned.

There was a long pause and then Nico spoke. "I'll do what I can. I just hope they're prepared for what it will take."

Cinder slid down the side of the wall until her knees were curled up to her chest. She hugged herself in consolation. The men's voices fell away from her ears now, and she felt the tears well over her eyelids and track down her face.

She was happy for Nico still being alive.

She was scared.

She was overwhelmed.

Her body didn't know how to process the onslaught of emotions other than to just cry.

She lifted her head and looked around the bare chamber. She had grown accustomed to tapestries, elegant pillows, jewels, and gifts from the prince... Donte, that always dotted the room. She remembered how the golden trinkets and baubles would gleam in the moonlight. When the Palace of Lazar was safe, they had all lived in peace. Would that day ever come again?

CINDER HAD FALLEN asleep on the floor of the chamber, beneath the window. When she heard the footsteps coming toward her, it broke her fitful rest, and she immediately noticed that the sun had not yet risen. Her eyes still filled with sleep, she sat up straight and began to take to her feet as Nico came toward her. For a moment, she considered rushing to him and embracing in a hug, but she could see that he meant business, and had been ordered by the prince to complete a task. She didn't want to get in the way of that. She had already caused the man such grief and had nearly gotten him killed.

"Ladies, forgive me for barging in. But there's

no time to waste. Can you all get ready please?" Nico asked, as he surveyed the waking harem.

The lanterns and candles had blown out while she had slept on the floor, and the room was still mostly dark, which she was grateful for. It didn't bother her that Nico had come in unannounced, but she didn't know how he would react to seeing her which it was clear he hadn't yet.

"There is no time to waste, ladies. Let's get moving," he said, as he approached Cinder and the women who slept near her.

"My name's Nico. I've been asked to help train you. I have a few others helping me and they're waiting in the courtyard for us." He reached for Cinder's silk wrap and handed it to her with a warm smile on his face. "Nice to see you again. I'm glad you survived. When I woke up after the attack, you were gone."

"Yes, they knocked me out, took me, and had me join the rest of the captured harem. We were rescued and brought here," she mumbled quietly, staring into his face like she had seen a ghost. His clothing was well-worn, with holes and rips in the light brown fabric. "I thought you were dead…"

"I thought the same about you," he said as his jaw clenched.

She wrapped her silk around herself and slipped into a pair of cloth shoes. Wishing for an

ivory comb, she had no choice but to use her
fingers. Quickly working them through her hair,
she untangled the knots that lingered at the tips. It
moved around her shoulders and as the first ray of
sunlight burst over the horizon, the orange aura
snuck into the room now. Its exposure cast light on
his face, and Cinder found herself staring at the
man she feared she had lost.

He glanced at her and all the other women
primping. "Your appearance is not of importance
now, ladies. Time's wasting." He walked to the
doorway and stopped under the archway while he
waited for all the women to stand ready.
"Follow me."

He walked with purpose down the long halls,
with the harem following in tow. As they passed
other chambers, she peeked inside each one to see
if she could get a glimpse of Donte. She saw no
one, and felt her anxiety grow because of it.

"Will we be waking this early every day for
our... lessons?" one of the women whined.

"Yes. There's no time to spare," he answered
curtly.

"So you continue to say," she replied, as they
walked the remainder of their short trip through
the housing unit and to the courtyard in silence.

Coming into the courtyard, Cinder saw some
other women of the harem who'd been staying in

another room. There were looks of fear and curiosity on their faces, and she made a direct line toward Elbi.

Elbi was sitting on the edge of a small wooden bench, smoking from a rolled paper, the tobacco stuck to her lower lip.

"Are you insane?" Cinder said, looking around to make sure no one saw what she was doing. "What would Donte say if he caught you?" Cinder warned her. "Or should I say, what would he *do* to you?"

Elbi's friendship was by far the most meaningful one that Cinder had. Especially after losing Maysa. Elbi, despite all her rigorous training and leveled expectation that she adapt to the submissive role of the harem, still had a wild streak in her. The wildness in her was a trait Cinder envied.

Elbi looked miserable, more so than the other women. She looked up at Cinder from her perch and gave her a lazy grin. "Luckily for me, he's planning our death sentence right now with the rest of the commanders."

Cinder sat on the ground, knees bent beside her. "I'm scared, Elbi. I probably shouldn't say that, but I am."

Elbi exhaled a large puff of smoke and gave a weak smile. "Yeah... I am too. We just need to do as they asked, and learn what we can."

"I guess we have no choice," Cinder said.

"Who's this guy Nico? We don't even know him. Why can't it be Donte or even one of the guards we already know? Why aren't they here?" Elbi stamped out her rolled cigarette in the sand and began to pick the loose leaves from her lips, spitting them messily onto the ground.

"We can trust Nico with our lives. I owe him mine. If it weren't for him, I would have been raped and killed."

Cinder stood and brushed the remnants of sand from her covered legs. The two women looked at the soldiers who began to file into the courtyard. Their presence ruffled the other harem women, and where once they had been tittering to each other like small hens, the footfall was enough to quiet them and push them into their respective roles.

"Something does seem to bother you," Cinder spoke out of the side of her mouth.

"It's nothing we need to discuss now," Elbi said. And before Cinder could prod any further, she stood up and walked away from her. It annoyed Cinder, but she was more curious than angry.

"Ladies, please if you would, come sit before me and my men," Nico commanded.

In the early morning light, she could see him

quite well. He was well-muscled but his face looked worn. There were small cracks in his otherwise chiseled face. The lines sat heavy around his eyes. His tattered clothing—which he was still wearing, she noticed, despite having to present himself in front of the entire harem—looked even thinner in the growing dawn. He wore a long scimitar on his hip. His shoulders were broad, and before she could really consider the narrowness of his hips, she felt eyes burning into her. She looked up to see that Elbi was staring at her from across the courtyard. She knew precisely what Cinder was prepared to admire, and she raised her eyebrows and winked at her, quick as lightning. Cinder shook off the suggestion and brought her eyes back around to Nico.

"My name's Nico, for those of you who have not met me yet. The Prince of Lazar, as I am sure you know, has instructed me and my men"—he waved his arm widely toward the men who had now formed a line, shoulder to shoulder—"to teach you the way of the warrior. You face dire times, and I'll not tell you a single lie. Should the Jaden army capture you, you'll wish yourself dead, as I'm sure many of you already know. But if you love your life, you'll listen to the teachings we have for you. And you'll obey."

Nico began to walk amongst the women,

carefully considering each one. Cinder looked to see if he had lust in his heart when he looked at them, but truthfully, if he did, she could not see it. This piqued her curiosity. A man who could walk amongst a bevy of beautiful women, especially women he had at his command, without so much as a hint of wanton desire, was a man in control of even the deepest, most primal parts of his being.

Cinder interrupted him, embarrassed by her meek, childish-sounding voice. "Where is Donte?"

"The prince is with his commanders this morning. They're busy making plans to better fortify Casen. We all take your safety very seriously."

"He won't be observing us?" Cinder's voice cracked. Her heart rate sped up. For some reason, the idea of going this long without Donte formed a panic in the depths of her belly. Or maybe it was seeing Nico again. Memories of death, the distant sound of barking dogs rang in her ear, and she could smell the metallic odor of blood once again.

"He needn't watch everything you do, Cinder," Mistress Tula said impatiently.

She hadn't seen Mistress Tula arrive. The woman stood with her arms crossed tightly against her chest and her lips formed in a firm line. "You will do as these men direct, or I will punish you. I'll not accept any disobedience from any of you."

Cinder looked at the ground in fear that she would otherwise glare in the woman's direction. It shamed her that she disliked Mistress Tula so much. Mistress Tula had been placed in charge, and Cinder was to respect her at all times, but she found it difficult. Cinder knew her place, however, and recoiled back into herself.

Nico moved forward. "What we will do today is learn the most preliminary measures of defense. You'll learn how to have the correct posture when you're being grabbed so that you may find a way out and free yourself. If you are unable to free yourself, we'll show you how to move your arms and legs in such a way that will harm or slow your captor. Do you all understand?"

The fifteen women nodded without saying a word. For each woman there was an assigned soldier and for a moment, Cinder wondered if Nico would be the one to work with her. He began to walk toward her, and she felt her stomach tighten. With subtlety, she eased her shoulders back and watched him as he approached. He looked at her, but she felt as though he was looking through her. Not seeing her. Another soldier stepped from behind Nico and moved toward her as Nico walked past and stood before Elbi. Cinder didn't dare look at him in that moment, and she didn't know why. She instead rested her eyes on the soldier before her, a younger man with a deep olive complexion and green eyes.

He smiled at her obligingly, giving her a brief nod of the head. " Ma'am."

"Cinder," she replied shortly, as she noticed Nico say something to Elbi and then quickly walk away.

Cinder looked at the soldier squarely. And so, the first morning of the harem's training commenced.

Trained first in positions and stances, the women felt shy and awkward. Their bodies were not accustomed to prolonged bouts of physical activity. Their life of leisure had kept them soft and supple. And, undoubtedly, their grooming and pampering had left them as real life works of art, more to be admired than handled.

But Nico walked around the women as they were propped up and guided, arms and legs poked and pulled into the right positions, and as the morning hours faded away into the afternoon, his voice grew louder and more forceful. To encourage their attention, he would tell them what they were up against, obviously hoping that fear would be the greater teacher of the day.

"Most of you have lived in Lazar for your entire adult lives, I'm told," he began. He circled around each woman as he continued. "You have no idea the battle we have in store to conquer Lazar. Though we will be there to try to protect you, we will be easily outmatched by Jaden warriors, three to one. We are lucky that our army is growing daily, by allied forces, but Jaden still has the upper hand. I'll tell you now what they will do."

Cinder hung on his every word. Before they'd left Lazar they were told of Jaden's murderous rages through the desert communes. It had seemed that with each commune conquered, they become more fearsome and bloodthirsty. They considered themselves, Cinder had heard, to be equalizers of the world's wrongs. She was inherently afraid of them.

Nico continued on. "There was a siege on the commune I lived at last. Jaden came running down the dunes, screaming shrill calls to each other. I watched as they picked off our men one by one. Their swords were guided with swift pursuit, and I watched them kill men who were easily bigger in size and by far the smartest men of the commune. But Jaden's swords cut through them at the neck. They had a thirst that my commune didn't know existed. It wasn't for precious water. It was for blood. We didn't see it coming. I watched blood stain the sand, and I saw men I called friends..." Nico's face contorted with the memory.

Cinder was surprised to see him show such

emotion now. He would stop every few moments and gaze at one of the women as she was held in a locked position by a soldier who would then guide her arm back and into a jabbing motion low into their guts.

"And then I saw them begin to pick off the women. The girls who were young and beautiful, as all of you are now, were slung over their shoulders after being grabbed or bludgeoned on the head and knocked out or nearly unconscious. I saw these men throw themselves on top of our young girls, raping them. I listened to the women scream and watched them bite, pinch and claw at these men. But nothing could stop them. When they were determined to have a woman, they would take her. I fought as best as I could with no weapons and no preparation. And then I saw something that convinced me my life would be dedicated to defeating men like these animals. These monsters of the desert. I saw a man who snuck up behind a girl a few years younger than all of you. She was crying, motionless, in a heap on the ground. He grabbed at her in his blind passion. He couldn't make contact with her without enduring her swipes to his face. And finally, when he had her wrapped in his arms, she bit down hard on his neck and drew blood from him. He screamed and let her go, throwing her to the ground, but not before slapping her across her face so hard that her nose began to spout blood. He was so enraged, he took her by her hair, swung her around and laid her out on the ground, flat on her face. Quicker than I could realize what he was about to do, he pulled his sword out, swung it around his own head and down on her neck. Her screaming stopped instantly, and what was once a farmer's daughter, was now little more than a head rolling away from her body. A headless body spilling crimson red."

The harem women had stopped in place. Their eyes were wide, their mouths slightly agape.

Cinder screamed, "Nico! That's enough!"

Cinder began to sob. Something inside her snapped. Whatever had been holding her fragile mind together, now crumbled. A deep well of madness took over. She had no choice but to leave the courtyard in a quick sprint.

"You don't want to hear this," Nico began, "but you need to know what it is you are up against." His voice faded as she ran—deeper, and deeper into the darkness.

22

"Come on, Cinder," Elbi pleaded, as she stood on the other side of the bathroom door. "It's okay to let me in. It's just me."

Cinder sat, blocking the door with her crumpled body on the floor, quickly running her hand through her brown hair. She held her hands close to her, afraid to let them be anywhere else. Her wide eyes tried to take in as much as possible and they kept darting around, taking in everything in the room. She could barely breathe. The pain in her chest made her wonder if she was dying of fright. Sweat formed on the top of her lip, yet she shook uncontrollably.

Elbi knocked on the door again. "Nico was just telling the story so all the women would take training seriously. Don't let what he said scare you.

Our situation is different. We will be prepared, so nothing bad will happen to us." She knocked on the door again. "Please let me in."

"Cinder," she heard a deep male voice call from the other side. "It's Donte. I'm coming in." Without waiting for a reply, he slowly opened the door, pushing against her body that sat against it.

Cinder looked up through her tears and began to cry even harder. Sobs rocked through her body as she gasped for whatever air her tightened lungs would accept. The ringing in her ears grew louder and darkness edged her vision.

"It's all right, Cinder," Donte said, as he carefully lowered himself to his knees. He extended two hands hesitantly. "Everything is going to be all right now. I want you to look me in the eyes and know that you are not in danger."

She did as he asked, looking into the depths of his blue eyes.

"I want you to take a deep breath and try to calm down." He turned to Elbi, who stood in the doorway with terror painted on her face. "Go get me a glass of water," he directed softly.

Cinder continued to look into his eyes and took a deep breath. The effort caused a pain in her back, and the tightness in her chest intensified.

"Good girl." He squeezed both of her hands, which were engulfed in his. "Now take another one. Focus on me and know I'm here and will not leave you."

She took another deep breath as Elbi came rushing back to the bathroom with water in hand. Donte released Cinder's hands and took the glass, gently placing it to her lips.

"Take a small sip," he said as he tilted the glass.

She once again followed his command and took a drink, coughing slightly when the water made its way to her tight throat. She took one more sip and felt her chest loosen up a bit. The ringing stopped, and her vision cleared somewhat.

He kissed the top of her hand. "Good girl. Calm down. I'm here." He returned the glass to Elbi. "I'll take it from here, Elbi. Please go and inform everyone that Cinder is fine, and I'll be attending to her this evening. Then get some help and bring back a few buckets of hot water, and leave them by the door."

Elbi nodded silently, gave her friend a soft smile, and turned to do as Donte asked.

Cinder covered her face with her hands, continuing to shake a little. She shook her head and let her sweaty locks spill everywhere. She had never been so embarrassed, so ashamed.

He let out a soft sigh. "Cinder, everything is going to be all right. You had a rough day and were pushed too far. You had a panic attack, and you'll feel much better once we calm you down."

She peeked out from behind her hands to look at him. "I'm so afraid. I'm not strong enough. I'm so sorry!" She began to cry even harder. "Maysa died because of me. She did, and I know that others will die too, and I can't stand the thought of seeing anyone else I know die."

"Look at me. Take another deep breath and look at me."

Cinder carefully lowered her hands from her face, trying to take deep, calming breaths.

"That's it," Donte said softly, extending a hand. "It is okay, Cinder. There is nothing to be ashamed of." The thick accent of his voice helped soothe her nerves. The way her name rolled off his tongue sounded like a soft lullaby. The pain in her chest continued to lessen.

Cinder's hand shook when he lifted it up and placed it in his palm. Her hand was sticky, sweaty with anxiety. He pulled her against his chest and just held her. Held her tightly against his body, allowing her to cling to his strength. They remained like that for quite some time, until they heard the sound of buckets being placed outside the door.

"Since we're here in the bathroom, let us get you a bath, shall we? We'll get you cleaned up."

Cinder froze when Donte grabbed the buckets of water for the bath and began to cry again.

"It's going to be all right. You need to calm down," he softly ordered.

She tucked her legs up to her chest and rested her forehead against her knees, her body continuing to tremble. Donte sat down on the edge of the tub and carefully rested a hand on her back.

"You can have trust in me, Cinder," he whispered. "You're not in danger anymore. I promise you that I'll not let you feel this afraid again." He turned to tend to the bath and said over his shoulder, "I'll give you some privacy to bathe, but I will be on the other side of the door, waiting."

She took a breath and raised her head, only for tears to start rolling down her cheeks in streams. "Please don't leave me."

"I'll only be on the other side of the door," he lightly encouraged. "I can go get Elbi if you want someone to be with you."

"Please stay with me," Cinder pleaded, letting a sob shake her body. She had just experienced the edge of insanity, and Donte was the only thing keeping her from falling into the abyss.

He stood up and wrung his hands together. "Very well. Let me help you undress and get into the bath."

Cinder's sobs stopped, and she glanced up at him. "Thank you," she whispered.

Silently, he stood her up and untied her soiled silk. She hadn't realized how filthy she truly was until that moment. She should have been embarrassed at her state of condition, but all she could feel was a sense of security.

Donte removed her clothing, baring her completely. He pulled her gently and assisted her balance as she stepped into the bath. His hands gently grasped her shoulders, lowering her down into the steaming water.

She let out a soft sigh when the water warmed the stiffness right out of her.

"Cinder," he said, so quietly she almost didn't hear him. "I am so sorry for everything you have been through. I take full responsibility. If I could take away all your fear, I would."

She allowed the remaining tears to silently fall down her face as Donte washed her hair. She needed to cry it all out. She needed to feel vulnerable, she needed to allow all her fear to surface. She wanted to be strong. She wanted to be the courageous fighter in battle, but at this moment in time, she was just a scared little girl.

Donte reached for a sponge and began washing her back, her shoulders, and then he gently placed the sponge to her face. He looked her in the eyes as he washed the tears from her cheeks.

"This won't be the last of our story. I swear you this."

The pain on his face pulled at her heart. She knew he meant it. But she didn't know if what he said was possible. All she could do was whisper, "Promise?"

He nodded with a soft smile. He leaned in and gently kissed the tip of her nose. "I promise."

Donte stood up and carefully assisted her out of the bath, dried her off and wrapped her in a large towel. He escorted her to the other room, closing the bathroom door behind them.

"I'm going to take you to my quarters to stay with me. Is that all right with you?"

"I don't want to be a burden to you. I'm sure you have your hands full with everything. The last thing you need right now is to be babysitting me." She tried to walk away, but her legs began to wobble, and she reached out for him to steady herself.

He quickly supported her weight. "You're exhausted, and you need to be watched over." He helped guide her to the hallway, where a worried Elbi stood with some others from the harem. "Will you ladies gather some fresh silks and overnight supplies for Cinder? She'll be residing in my quarters until further notice."

A relief washed over Cinder that almost set her heart rate at normal pace. Donte's take-charge attitude was the only thing making her feel like she wasn't drowning in a sea of terror. She glanced at Elbi, and suddenly felt guilty for making her friend worry so much. She bowed her head in shame and allowed her damp hair to cascade forward around her face, forming a curtain of disguise.

When Elbi left and the other girls followed, he tilted her face so she had no choice but to look into his eyes. He brushed her hair away from her face and said, "I will never allow you to have another panic attack. I will never allow you to feel such fear. I will be here. Trust in that."

"Everyone else can handle it. No one else is panicking. I'm the weak link and simply holding you, and everyone around me, down. I feel so ashamed."

"There is no shame in truth, Cinder. You only express the truth that every single person at Casen is feeling. Everyone is afraid. We are all scared. Just because you are the most honest person here, does not mean you are the weakest." Donte wrapped his arm around her body and pulled her close to him as he guided her down the hallway. "With a little rest, you'll be ready to face your truth head on."

23

Night had fallen when her eyes finally fluttered open, the smell of roasting meat catching her attention first, followed by something soft beneath her. She looked around, her eyes adjusting to the flickering candlelight after a moment, and as they did acclimate, she realized she had been carried to Donte's bedroom. The bed beneath her was covered with a fur-lined blanket, which was brightly colored, and warm. She stretched only a small bit before pushing herself up, combing her fingers through her hair and scrubbing the dried tears from her eyes. It smelled like him, the bed; a fragrance that set her soul at ease but her heart aflutter. She blushed at the thought of what they could do in this bed, but reminded herself that there was no shame in it, since he was, after all, Donte of Lazar.

Standing up, she straightened the blanket and pillows beneath her on the bed before she found her way back out into the other room, where a fire burned and a pot bubbled away, full of some thick stew. She was surprised, as she didn't know many men who could cook anything, let alone what she saw over the fire. She found a large wooden spoon and gave the pot a stir before she found a towel and pulled a pan of biscuits off, setting them carefully on the table. She looked around the little place, which clearly had only those two rooms. Still, it was well-built, and neatly kept, save for some dust, which she expected was impossible to keep out. It was nowhere near as impressive as the accommodations of the Palace of Lazar, but it was still cozy and welcoming. Elegance and opulence were replaced by quaint and inviting.

The only thing missing was Donte. As if the thought had drawn him in, the door opened and swung closed as the handsome man stepped in, carrying an armful of freshly split firewood. He paused when he saw that she was awake before putting the wood near the fire, turning to look at her in silence for a moment before he spoke, at last.

"Did you sleep well?"

She nodded gently, fidgeting with the edge of her silk. "Yes, thank you."

"How are you feeling? Has all the tightness in your chest gone away?"

"It has." She thought for a moment, chewing her lip, before she added, "I'm sorry to be such a burden. I feel much better, and can join the rest of the harem now."

He paused a moment, nodding slowly. "If that is what you truly want." Then he crossed the room and cupped his hands on both sides of her face. "But *is* it truly what you want?"

She tried to turn her head away, but he held it firmly in place. Averting her eyes, she said, "I don't want to make my problems yours."

"Look at me," he commanded.

She did as he directed.

With his hands still cupped on her face, he asked, "Do you want to stay with me? Or do you want to join the harem?"

"I feel safer with you."

"Then the decision is made. You'll stay with me until we return to Lazar."

"The entire time?" His declaration surprised her. She didn't know what to make of it.

He smiled, his eyes reflecting the firelight, the flames dancing in them. "Yes, the entire time." He let go of her face and turned toward the meal, stirring as he spoke. "My quarters are small, but secure. As long as I'm here, you are protected. And when I am not here, I'll make sure you are still protected." He turned to look at her with another reassuring smile. "I promised you that you would always feel safe. I plan to honor my word."

There was an awkward silence between them, neither seeming to know what to say. He was the first to break it, moving to gather a couple of plates so they could have dinner. "I would like you to continue to train with Nico and his men during the day. He has assured me that he will keep his tales to a limit from now on." Donte smirked and gave her a playful wink.

She nodded. "Yes, sir. I'm sorry I ran out like that. I really made a fool of myself. Here, let me," she went on, moving to stand in front of the fire, taking the plates from him. She didn't like standing around doing nothing the whole time while he was on his feet; it didn't feel right to her.

He relinquished the plates and instead took a seat at the table, reaching up and rubbing at the back of his neck. "I don't want to hear you talk about yourself in such a manner again. You are not a fool. Fools are people who have no fear at all. Fools are people who don't approach life with caution. Fools are people who confuse bravery with thoughtlessness. You, Cinder, are not a fool."

Placing both the plates, now filled with food, onto the table and sitting down across from him, she frowned. "What will people say about me staying with you? It's not the way of the harem."

He shook his head, picking up his spoon and shoveling a mouthful of vegetables in before he continued. "The ways of the harem will need to adapt."

"What about the rest of the women? Where will they stay?"

He paused from eating and studied her face in silence for several moments. "The rest of the women will be housed in the main building, under intense security. They'll train every day just as you will. Which leads me to my next discussion." He motioned for her to start eating, which she quickly did. "You are to go nowhere without my permission."

She swallowed the bite of delicious, savory meat and nodded. She knew better than to argue, although she was slightly curious as to why.

"When you are with me, it is my responsibility to protect you. The majority of the soldiers are guarding the women in the main building. Therefore, you are to remain by my side until I hand you over to training with Nico. I will then pick you up at the day's end, and you'll return to my quarters. You are never to leave, or wander without me. Understood?"

Up until now, he'd been very gentle with her since her panic attack, his voice soft, understanding. These harsh tones concerned her greatly, and she wasn't sure how to react to them. "I... Yes. I understand." She wasn't sure why he was so adamant, but she hoped he didn't plan on keeping her locked up inside his quarters all the time.

He nodded, tucking into his meal and falling silent for the moment. That silence seemed to stretch, unending, between them like an ever-deepening chasm. He finished his meal after several minutes and leaned back, rubbing his hand over his chest with a yawn. "I suppose it's time we get some sleep. You've been through a lot today, and more training is ahead for tomorrow."

She quickly stood up and cleared the dishes. "Oh, I see..." She thought for a moment, unsure if she was supposed to follow him, or if she should stay awake and get better acquainted with her new home. "Would you like me to come with you?" She wasn't sure what was expected of her. The rules had changed, but was she still expected to perform harem duties?

He paused at the question for a moment. "Yes, I would," he answered finally, standing and holding his hand out to her as he came around the table, a sweet smile on his face.

Her heart melted when she saw the gentle way he looked at her, the kindness in his blue eyes. He truly was a handsome man. She laid her hand in his and let him lead her back into the bedroom where she'd recently awakened.

He closed the door behind him and, leaving her to linger there, moved to sit on the bed and pull off his boots. His shirt was unbuttoned, tossed aside, as well as his socks. She noticed, however, that he didn't remove all of his clothes.

Cinder walked over to the bed and turned down the covers for him, sitting down for a moment to pull off her own shoes, and finally her silks, until she sat completely nude. Nothing out of the ordinary for a harem girl, but somehow it felt different now. She blushed a bit as she climbed into the bed, tugging the covers up over herself and taking a deep breath. Any art of seduction training had been thrown out the window. She had no idea what to do. She reminded herself that she was his now, and that if he wanted something from her... well, it was her place to give it to him. Her training had prepared her for this, or at least it was supposed to.

He blew the candle out, turning to face her as he lay down and pulled the blanket up. He slid a little closer, until she could feel the warmth of his body. His hand moved around her waist, gently pulling her closer so her back was pressed against his chest, his arm over her.

She shivered when he held her like that. It felt so warm, so nice. She knew he would be gentle, firm, but kind with her. She could sense something in the way he held her, so protectively, that he would never do her harm.

She waited for the next move.

When none followed, she wondered if she was the one supposed to make the move. Her question was soon answered by the heavy breathing of Donte against the back of her head. Taking a moment to relish the weight of his sleeping body pressed against hers, she eventually closed her eyes and drifted off into sleep, tightly wrapped in his arms as the moon slowly sank and gave way to the sun.

The desert, through the bedroom window, was beautiful in the sunrise, casting its glow over the earth from its fiery throne in the sky. Like a great burning eye in the heavens, it watched over those below, giving life to all under its rule.

When Cinder fully awoke, she found an empty space beside her. It took her a few moments to remember the events of the previous day, to remember how she'd ended up in Donte's bed.

How warm he was, how soft, how protective... She bolted upright, immediately stricken with a deep fear that something had happened to him, however irrational it might have been.

She jumped from the bed and ran into the other room, her heart pounding when she did not see him there either. The fire roared behind her, a skillet sizzled with eggs and the smell of biscuits greeted her nose. The door opened and he stepped in, momentarily silhouetted by the sunlight, which cast a halo about his head like some angelic figure. Cinder relaxed somewhat, wondering what she must look like, standing there wide-eyed and naked. She was so quick to jump the gun, to let her mind wander to the worst of possibilities.

"Good morning," Donte greeted, granting her a wide smile that made her heart skip a little beat. He scanned her body and said, "We have a busy day ahead. Go get dressed and come have some breakfast. I'll then escort you to training."

24

The hot afternoon sun began to bake the courtyard, and the women were growing both physically and mentally exhausted with their lesson. Even the men had soaked through their uniforms with sweat, and though they did not let on that they were frustrated with what little progress the harem had made, Cinder, between her attempts at jabbing her soldier and breaking free of his grasp, could sense their growing impatience.

Mistress Tula, Mistress Krin, and Mistress Lana also looked less than pleased as they sat in a shadowy part of the courtyard, watching them all with scrutiny. Why the three sisters weren't expected to train, Cinder didn't know. But she hated the way the women watched her.

"I cannot do any more of this today," Elbi said,

and she stepped away from her trainer immediately. "I don't feel well."

"All right, ladies. That's enough for today," Nico gave in.

The women let out a collective breath and began to walk their glistening bodies and damp heads of hair out of the courtyard. All of them were bedraggled. They were also emotionally spent.

Cinder hung back. She watched Elbi stretch her aching back, and believed she could see her crying. The soldiers were now on the far side of the courtyard, standing in the shade of an old date palm and chatting to each other. Cinder walked over to Elbi and touched the small of her back.

"Elbi, are you sick? What's wrong?" she asked, her brow furrowed in genuine concern.

Elbi cast her eyes down to her feet and shook her head with a mixture of agony and anger.

"I'm not sick. I'm just tired of waking up and preparing for war, then having nightmares about war, then waking up and starting the whole cycle again." Her hair stuck to her forehead with sweat, but she still exuded a beauty that made Cinder jealous. "I overhear the soldiers talking and what they say is terrifying."

Cinder's heart stopped. "What... what do they say?"

Elbi opened her mouth to tell her and then

shook her head. She began to whip around and walk away, but Cinder deftly snatched her wrist and pulled her back.

The soldiers had noticed the exchange all at once and looked curiously over at the two women. Nico pardoned himself and walked over to them. "Is there a problem, ladies?" he asked.

Somewhat ashamed, Cinder felt her cheeks brighten and she let go of Elbi's wrist. Though she was embarrassed, she knew that Elbi would open up to her eventually. She would get her alone, and she would find out what was really in store for them.

"Let me handle this," Mistress Tula said as she came up from behind. "It's my job to oversee the harem's behavior and well-being. If Elbi is ill, I shall attend to her."

Elbi quickly shook her head. "I'm not ill. I just—"

"You had the training stopped because you declared you were ill." Mistress Tula grabbed Elbi's arm and started to pull her toward the main building. "Come with me." She paused and looked over her shoulder. "Cinder, I think you should come as well. I want to make sure you have not caught anything from your friend."

She followed Mistress Tula—albeit reluctantly

—to the main building. This wasn't going to end well; Cinder knew that much.

As they entered the living quarters, Mistress Tula ordered, "Remove your silks, find a corner and kneel in it. I'll return in a moment."

The women gave each other a knowing look. Both quickly removed their clothing, as ordered, and kneeled in separate corners, as close together as possible so they could still converse.

"Where do you think she went?" Cinder whispered, feeling the cooler air of the room against her naked skin.

"I don't know. But I don't have a good feeling about this."

The door opened and Cinder could hear Mistress Tula dragging something into the room. It sounded heavy and bulky by the way the woman was huffing and puffing. Cinder wanted to turn around, but didn't dare. She had been on too many receiving ends of Mistress Tula's wrath. So instead, she pressed her nose closer to the dusty corner. She hoped Mistress Tula would appreciate her compliant, good girl behavior.

Goosebumps covered her skin as a chill worked up Cinder's spine. Part of it was the temperature of the barren room, and the other part was in anticipation of what was to come.

"Elbi, come over here and lie on the table. Put

your feet in the stirrups. Cinder, you can come over and watch while you wait your turn."

As they turned from their corner, Cinder saw that Mistress Tula had brought in an exam table and a tray of tools.

"Do not look so surprised. The prince was planning on turning Casen into a secondary harem until the war with Jaden hit. So there are some necessary harem training tools here. I believe an exam should have been performed on every harem girl upon entering Casen, but for now we will start with Elbi."

Elbi quickly did as she was asked. The harem girl training in her was still very clear.

Cinder went and stood next to the table as directed by Mistress Tula's hand gesture.

Mistress Tula gloved up and spread Elbi's legs even more. "Scoot your bottom to the edge."

Elbi did as she asked, glanced at Cinder and then closed her eyes. Her face was bright red, and she grimaced as the first implement went inside her. Cinder didn't want to look at the metal tools going into Elbi's vagina. They scared her, and since she was probably next, she really didn't want to know what was going to go inside her own body. Some things were better not known.

After a few moments, Mistress Tula broke the silence. "You are not a virgin anymore! And I know everyone the prince has ever been with sexually, and neither of you are on that list!"

Elbi sat up instantly, looking stunned at the accusation.

"You are no harem girl! You'll be cast off from here!" Mistress Tula stood up, with fury burning in her eyes. She looked over at Cinder. "Are you still a virgin?" The anger made the woman look crazy.

Cinder nodded enthusiastically. "Yes, Mistress Tula." Panic sank in, and she had no choice but to lie. She was too scared to admit the truth. Cinder wasn't sure what all this meant that Elbi wasn't a virgin... had she also had sex with Donte?

Intense jealousy took over.

No. Not with Donte. He was hers! Hers!

But was he?

She looked at Elbi, who still sat with her mouth open and eyes wide.

"Elbi, stand up and lean over the bed this instant!"

Elbi quickly scrambled off the exam table and leaned over as directed. She stuck her bottom out —she was no novice to being punished. Mistress Tula walked over to a trunk against the wall and pulled out a leather belt. Cinder swallowed back her fear. She was about to watch her friend get whipped by a belt.

Mistress Tula wasted no time and offered no

warm up. She rained lash after lash of the belt on a howling Elbi. She offered no mercy as the welts criss-crossed poor Elbi's ass. Elbi rose on her toes and screamed out with every whip of the belt.

Cinder had never seen anyone punished so severely. Over and over, the belting continued. Cinder cried for her friend and struggled not to step in to save her. She stood helpless, not sure what to do. Not sure if she was next. Not sure of anything except that her friend was getting the punishment of a lifetime. Elbi screamed and pleaded, begging for mercy. But Mistress Tula continued. Just when Cinder was going to run screaming from the room for help, as foolish as that might have been, the beating ended.

"Both of you get on your arms and knees. Face down and asses high in the air. Now!" she screeched, when Cinder and Elbi hesitated.

The two women did as she asked, never glancing at each other for fear of what Mistress Tula would do. Cinder knew what this position meant. Something was going to happen anally. Any question of that was quickly remedied by Mistress Tula walking around them.

"You girls must be cleansed. Clearly it's overdue." And with that, a nozzle for an enema was shoved into Cinder's tight hole. She couldn't help but cry out. Mostly due to the surprise, but also because it appeared no lubrication was used, and the entrance past her puckered skin wasn't very smooth. Elbi gasped a second later, as the same intrusion happened to her.

Mistress Tula started to pump the nozzle in and out of Cinder's dry anus. By the sounds of Elbi, it seemed as if Mistress Tula was doing the same to her with her other hand. She was relentlessly ass fucking both of them with the enema nozzles.

"You will take these enemas while I go find the prince and tell him of Elbi's deflowering." Mistress Tula punctuated each word of her sentence with a thrust of the dry nozzle. Each aggressive thrust rubbed Cinder's puckered hole raw. She gasped and wiggled, but she tried her best to take the invasion without complaint for fear that she, too, would get a belting.

Mistress Tula stood and turned on the enemas. It wasn't long before the cool fluid began to enter Cinder's channel. She hated enemas, but if this meant no more ass fucking by a plastic nozzle, then she was happy to receive it.

"I'll be back. Neither one of you move, or a whipping will follow." Footsteps were all that could be heard until the closing of the door.

As the door closed, Cinder asked, "Elbi, are you all right?" Elbi was only inches from her, so she didn't have to speak very loudly.

Elbi lifted her tear-stained face and said, "Yes. I'll be fine."

"I've never seen someone get punished so badly. Are you in pain?"

Elbi shook her head. "I'm fine. Please don't worry." She grimaced as no doubt the cramping in her lower belly began—as it did with Cinder.

Cinder moaned, suddenly wanting to evacuate her bowels. She breathed through it and tried to continue talking. "You aren't a virgin?" She couldn't help but worry whether Elbi would indeed be cast out. She also didn't want to picture Elbi being with Donte intimately.

Having his baby.

Being... his.

Did he claim Elbi as his just as he did with Cinder?

Did he say that to all the women of the harem?

"No, I'm not. My virginity and my body belong to one of the head guards of the palace. He's one of Prince Donte's commanders now." She smiled and huffed. "I don't even care anymore. I love him. So if I get cast out for love, then so be it."

Cinder released a breath she hadn't realized she'd been holding.

Thank God. Thank fucking God. Elbi did not lose her virginity to Donte.

"Well, why didn't you say anything? Why didn't

you stop her from whipping you?" Cinder couldn't believe what she was hearing. Elbi was in love, and prepared to face whatever consequences were in store.

"I was shocked. I wasn't prepared to tell anyone. And I wasn't sure if the commander wanted the information to be shared. He's so busy with the war preparations that I don't believe he has told Prince Donte yet. Maybe he has. I just don't know, so I remained quiet."

The fluid seemed to stop flowing from the nozzle in her ass, but that meant it was all inside her now. The cramping grew worse, and Cinder needed to release the pressure soon. She rocked from side to side and moaned. She couldn't focus on Elbi anymore. Just when she thought she couldn't take it any longer, Cinder reached under her body and began rubbing her lower abdomen. The position was awkward, since she was still on all fours, but she had to something.

"Just take deep breaths," Elbi soothed. The massage seemed to help—but not enough.

"Ahhh I can't! I can't hold it any longer." Cinder panicked. She knew that if she released her enema, a belt lashing would follow. And she knew she was not nearly as strong as Elbi in taking severe correction. Clenching her bottom only made the nozzle of the enema feel more intense. But if she didn't, she feared what would happen.

Cinder removed her hand quickly when the door suddenly opened. Mistress Tula came storming in and placed two buckets in front of both of them. "Evacuate your bowels in the buckets. Two guards are on the other side of the door to take you both back to your quarters." She walked away and back to the door. "Training to be a soldier or not, there are rules of the harem. Remember that." The door slammed closed behind her.

Cinder didn't waste any time, nor did Elbi. They both sat on their buckets and allowed the explosive release. Even though Cinder was doing this in front of her friend, the humiliation was excruciating. She tried not to look at Elbi, even though their buckets were almost touching.

As they both exited the room in shame, neither said a word to each other. Cinder had no choice but to head to Donte's quarters and hope this incident would just disappear.

25

"**T**hank you for bringing her home," Donte told the soldier escorting her to the door.

"Not a problem, sir." The soldier started to walk away, then stopped and turned around. "There was an incident between her and Elbi you may want to talk to her about," he said, crushing any chance Cinder had of hiding it from Donte. "I do believe Mistress Tula handled it, though."

Donte tilted his head and examined Cinder, who'd suddenly frozen in her spot. "Thank you again for escorting her home." He then reached for her hand and pulled her inside the small quarters.

She glanced down and blushed, reaching up to tuck a piece of hair behind her ear.

"Would you like to tell me what happened today?" he asked, wasting no time.

She took a deep breath and decided that the only chance of this evening ending well was to be honest. "Elbi ended training because she said she didn't feel well, but when I asked her about it, she said she was fine. But then she told me she had heard some scary information while eavesdropping on some soldiers, and I was trying to find out what it was." Cinder realized she'd been holding her breath while telling the story, and forced herself to exhale slowly. She knew she was rambling, but she was trying to say as much as she could before losing her courage. "I guess we got the attention of Nico and Mistress Tula, and well..." She took another deep breath. "Mistress Tula took us to the main building."

"For what purpose?" Donte walked over to a chair and sat down, a contemplative look on his face.

"To examine Elbi, to make sure she wasn't ill."

"Why did she have you come along?"

"She wanted to make sure I didn't catch anything from Elbi, I guess."

"Is that all?"

"No. Mistress Tula discovered that Elbi was no longer a virgin. She whipped... actually, more like beat Elbi for it. She then made Elbi and me wait while receiving an..." Cinder couldn't get out the last word. Humiliation washed over her.

Donte raised an eyebrow, anger clearly forming on his face. "What? While receiving what?"

"An... an enema." If embarrassment could kill, Cinder would be dead. "She told us she was looking for you to tell you the news about Elbi."

He slammed his hand down on the table and stood there, with fury in his eyes. Cinder took a few steps back in fear.

"I want you to lock the door behind me and stay here. Do not leave or allow anyone in. Do not defy me!" he shouted, heading for the door without any explanation, slamming it behind him.

Cinder was mortified at his reaction, brought to tears even, when he stormed from the quarters and left her alone. She sat down on the end of the bed, her fingers trembling with fright. What had she done so wrong? Surely, he was upset with her now. She could only hope that whatever punishment he decided to dole out to her for her wrongdoing would not be too harsh. And what of poor Elbi? Was he on his way to banish her from Casen? Where would she go? What would she do?

She buried her face in her hands, doing her best to quiet her tears, to stop their flow. Her shoulders shook gently, all the shame and humiliation from the day rushing at her all at once. She did not hear him come back into the room, nor did she hear the soft groan of the door as he opened it over the sounds of her own sobs.

The next thing she knew, his arms were wrapped around her, pulling her against his body, stroking her hair, soothing her. Her hands pressed to his chest, her cheek against his shoulder, she continued to cry, unable to stop.

"I didn't mean to upset you. I'm sorry," he said, his voice strong and smooth as he held her. "Seeing you crying like this breaks my heart to know I caused it. I never meant to frighten you. It was the last thing I wanted. I lost my temper, and I am sorry for that."

"It's all right. I am sorry for getting in trouble." She sniffled, feeling quite foolish for being so upset over something like this. She really did want to work on not crying all the time.

"No, it is not all right. Mistress Tula had no place, or directive, to do what she did. And you are mine to handle, not Mistress Tula's."

She looked up at him, her face streaked with tears, her eyes still glistening. "I belong to you? Not the harem? Am I not to follow the rules of the harem?"

Donte nodded. "As long as you reside with me and are under my protection, yes." He reached down and rubbed his thumb over her cheeks, wiping away the stray tears that threatened to fall from them.

She sighed gently when he touched her face, looking at him with compassion, taking his hand in hers and lacing their fingers. "Am I in trouble? Are you going to discipline me?"

"Do you believe you did anything to be disciplined for?"

Cinder shook her head. "No. It was confusing why we were being punished by Mistress Tula."

"Then of course I am not going to punish you."

She bit her lower lip, her eyes drifting to the floor. "But you were angry with me. You shouted and left."

He stroked her hair with the back of his hand. "I was angry with Mistress Tula and left to address the situation with my commander." Cinder looked at him with her eyes wide. "He is not pleased either and will be handling it," he added. "I knew of Elbi's situation, and though I wasn't pleased at first to hear of one of my guards being intimate with one of the harem girls, I don't hold it against either of them now. Hell, in this dark world, we need some romance and love around us."

Cinder felt complete relief in knowing her friend wouldn't be banished or even punished for her love affair. Prince Donte was clearly a merciful ruler, and for that, she was grateful.

Her gaze met his just moments before she found her lips captured in a passionate kiss. She had never been kissed before. Not like this, at least. His mouth pressed firmly, dominating hers as only Donte could do, but his tongue pushed past her lips with the gentlest entrance, softly dancing against hers. She returned the kiss with the same level of passion. Not because it was her duty to do so. Not because she was a harem girl trained to please her master, but because she had never wanted something like this before. Something so simple and yet so powerful at the same time.

26

The sun broke over the horizon, casting a gauzy yellow glow over the earth below. Birds preened in their nests atop the house, their shrill chirp more than enough to wake her. Cinder was getting used to being up early and, though her body screamed in defiance, the sunlight woke her nonetheless. She felt something warm over her hip, something heavy. Tilting her head, she glanced downward, seeing a tanned arm tossed over her. A smile graced her lips, her teeth scraping over them with a sigh.

She reached down and gently removed his hand from her hip, sliding the cover down so she could sit up. Just as her cheek lifted from the pillow, she felt something wrap around her waist, pulling her back down, pressing her against that warm, hard chest. She couldn't help the smile that crossed her face, the little giggle that escaped her lips when she felt his kisses on her shoulder.

"Good morning," she breathed, his touch sending a thrill through her that she struggled, in her inexperience, to hide.

"Good morning." His voice sounded so smooth, so easy, so different than it had the day before when he'd been angry with Mistress Tula. "How did you sleep?"

"Fine... I slept fine. I, uh, I am going to go make some breakfast." She wasn't ungrateful for how sweet he was being to her, quite the opposite in fact, but she was very confused about how to act the next morning. She pulled away from him, sitting up and seeing her silk where she'd left it lying the night before. She stood and dressed quickly, rushing from the room as her cheeks began to burn red, leaving him as fast as possible to hide her awkward embarrassment.

Soon the smell of bacon and coffee assaulted her nose, her stomach growling to remind her of how little she'd eaten the night before, but she didn't worry about it right now. No, she had other things on her mind.

At the sound of the bedroom door opening, Cinder looked over her shoulder to see Donte casually leaning against the frame. His eyes were fixed on her, her every movement, he seemed to be mesmerized by her. She blushed at the silent attention.

She offered a sheepish smile as the blush grew on her cheeks. "Breakfast will be ready soon."

He nodded at her, starting towards the door without any hesitation. "I'll be back shortly. I'm going to inform Nico that the harem needs a day of rest from training. I don't want exhaustion to take over. Plus, my commander has items he needs to address, as do I. I won't be long, stay inside," he warned again before he disappeared out the door, leaving her standing alone.

She desperately wanted to go outside and find Elbi, but she couldn't risk it. She was dying to know what had happened with the commander and Mistress Tula, but if Donte's concerns were well-founded—well, she didn't want to die by having a Jaden spy or assassin get her. She resigned herself to staying put. For now, she would busy herself cleaning his quarters, and feeding him the best breakfast she could. She went right to work on the dishes, setting everything she'd cooked out on the table, before turning to the basin where a few dirty plates still lay. She searched the room for a bucket of water, but found none, much to her dismay.

Cinder vaguely remembered seeing a well outside, near the door, and made up her mind, forgetting his warning in her haste, to go and get the water herself. She collected an empty bucket she found and opened up the door, stepping out into the little yard in front of the quarters. Her eyes took in the large desert dunes in the distance, silhouetted in the early morning sunlight, expanding as far as she could see.

She found the well not too far from the door, and before very much time had passed, she had drawn herself a bucketful of water that would be sufficient to clean the dishes inside the room. Hefting it up by the rope, which bit terribly into her delicate fingers, she carried it back inside the quarters, pausing only to collect a few desert flowers which were growing near the door to liven the place up.

It was some time before Donte returned, a bit more tense than he'd been before he left, and obviously hungry. He didn't waste any time moving over to the table and making himself a plate, offering her a wide smile as she came to sit across from him, until he saw the flowers in her hand, which she was arranging in a little jar she'd found.

"What are those?"

"They're flowers," she replied with a smile, arranging them in the jar carefully, sprucing them a bit. "Aren't they lovely?"

"I can see that they are flowers, but where did

you get them?" he demanded, his voice carrying a sharp edge to it that made her tense up.

"I... I found them. They were growing near the door."

"Outside? You went out there by yourself? After I told you not to!" He slammed his fist down on the table hard enough to make her jump, standing up abruptly, obviously very upset that his only request had been so blatantly disobeyed.

"I... I went to get some water... to wash the dishes. I didn't go far. I'm sorry. I—"

He cut her off again, before she could finish. "Do you realize how dangerous that was? There wasn't a soldier guarding you. If a Jaden soldier had been hiding in the dunes, that would have been the perfect time to strike and kidnap you. I told you how important it was for you to stay inside," he growled. He closed his eyes, took a deep breath and lowered himself back down into the chair. "Do you understand how the thought of that terrifies me?" he asked, in a much calmer tone.

Cinder wrung her hands in front of her. "You're right. I'm sorry. I guess I was enjoying playing house with you so much, I forgot that we are at war."

"Forgetting such a thing will get you killed!" His deep voice caused her to jump. "This isn't the palace anymore. This is not a safe haven for you to have a momentary lapse." He stood up from his meal, walked toward her, and stopped mere inches from her face. She wanted to look at him, but his intimidation caused her to look at the ground, fidgeting with her hands in front of her.

He stood there as if waiting for her to continue her excuse, but she had no reply. What could she say? She knew he was right, which just proved she wasn't meant to be in a battle-torn world. She had no chance of surviving.

"Cinder..."

She remained silent, not wanting to look into his disappointed eyes.

"Do you stand there in silence in defiance? Are you angry at my zealous dictates?"

She shook her head, but still remained silent as she stared at her bare toes peeking out from underneath her silks.

"Look at me."

She refused.

"I said, look at me." He tilted her chin up with his finger until she was staring up into his eyes.

His look of displeasure filled her with guilt. She wasn't a fighter, and now she couldn't even please the prince with her harem skills. She had been groomed to be obedient, compliant, and certainly to follow the commands of the prince. She had failed.

"What has you in tears, Cinder? A simple scolding can't have you so upset." She hadn't realized that tears were streaming down her face until that moment. "Are you afraid of me?" he asked, with concern in his voice.

She shook her head.

"Then what has you in tears? Answer me. I won't tolerate this act of silence any longer." Although his voice was firmer, there was still an underline of concern mixed with it.

"I'm not meant to survive. I feel as if I should have died in the desert by the hand of General Rhys or the attackers before that and saved the time of the inevitable."

Donte remained silent. Anger sizzled across his face as his eyes seemed to darken to a deeper shade of rich blue.

"What you require of us, I simply can't do." She wiped her nose with the arm of her sleeve as she continued to cry, simple tears now turning into small sobs. "I'm scared, I'm weak, I'm lost!" she said, with a sob that shook her shoulders.

Donte pulled her gently against his chest, and held her firmly, soothing her until she dried her tears and sniffed back the last of her momentary breakdown. As he spoke, his voice reverberated against her ear. "That's what I am here for. If you're scared, I'll protect you. If you're weak, I'll make you strong. As for being lost... explain that in more detail."

She hesitated in answering him, not sure what she truly meant by that statement. Or more so, not knowing how to verbalize it.

"Cinder..." The one word came clearly as a warning. She didn't know Donte well, but she knew enough to know his patience with her game of silence was wearing thin.

She should have answered him. The harem girl in her should have... but she remained trapped in her own silence.

Donte pulled away enough so that he was able to start lowering her silk. "I've had enough of your disrespect. When I ask you questions, I expect the courtesy of an answer. You can answer me, or be punished for defiance."

The harem girl should have answered right away and apologized for her behavior. But Cinder realized at that moment that the harem girl in her was what was lost.

"Very well," he said, as he tugged at the last knot holding her silk tight. Once that had been loosened, her clothing fell to the ground, exposing her completely. "You have made your choice."

The harem girl in her should have responded with a 'yes, sir' but once again, she held her tongue.

The harem girl was somewhere else... mislaid in the desert.

"Since you have nothing to say to me, then maybe a trip over my lap will help you find your voice." He pulled her with him to a modest wooden chair by the table in the middle of the room, still covered with what should have been a pleasant breakfast. In one effortless motion, he draped Cinder across his knee, readying her body for a punishment.

The harem girl in her should have submitted willingly, mentally preparing for the correction in store. But that did not happen. Instead, she tensed and tried to get up. Her heart was beating so fast and hard, she almost wondered if it could be heard by Donte. She was no stranger to discipline, submission and dominance. She knew how to be submissive... and yet... she didn't want to be.

He pressed her back down firmly and trapped her legs between his, then grabbed both of her hands and pinned them behind her lower back with one of his. If she wouldn't willingly give her submission, he was clearly about to force it.

As she stared at the wooden floor only a few inches from her face, she challenged his hold. She wiggled and bucked, trying her best to break free. Could she escape if she really wanted to?

Her answer was a sharp slap to her bare ass. It

stung, but for some reason she didn't want him to know it did. Another swat landed on one cheek and then another. Donte continued the spanking at a fast pace, but Cinder refused to gasp, plead or cry any further. She may not have control over her life, but she had control over her emotions with this discipline. She decided that she would take this punishment with grace and dignity. Donte had already seen enough tears from her.

He issued the slaps to her ass in silence. There was no lecture, no words of disapproval, just the sound of his hand peppering her rear with a growing force. Her bottom was on fire, and yet her eyes remained as dry as the desert. The pain grew as the spanking intensified, but she took the discipline in the most stoic of ways. A hive of stinging bees overtook her sensitive flesh as swat after swat landed on her upturned ass, and yet not a single gasp or moan escaped her lips. Not until the lecture began.

"It's all right to be scared. It is all right to feel weak." The punishment continued between his words. "If you're lost, then we'll find you." As hard as Cinder was trying not to let the spanking affect her, the pain escalated to a new level. "But I will not let you lose your spirit. I will not allow you to demean yourself and think less of who you are. You are a fighter, Cinder! Only the strong have survived, and you are alive!" The palm of Donte's hand came down with such ferocity over and over, that she had no choice but to release a wail of pain —but she would not let any tears come. She would hold on to that sign of weakness. "You will become stronger every single day, and we *will* make a warrior of you. I have no doubt that one is hidden behind the surface of this scared little girl."

His final words were the key to the floodgates. An explosion of sadness escaped. Yes, she was a scared little girl—terrified, in fact. So, allowing that little girl to be just that, she cried. She cried and cried and cried. She mourned her safety. She grieved for the life she so desperately missed. Cinder wept over the loss of Lazar. She allowed every ounce of sadness to leave her body via her tears and cries of pain.

Somewhere during the sobbing, Donte had stopped spanking her and pulled her up into his arms. She had no idea when or how that happened. It wasn't until her entire body hurt with the shaking of her gut-wrenching cries, and her body had no more to give, that she paused long enough to take in her surroundings.

She was covered in sweat, tears and snot. Her fiery ass pulsated against Donte's lap as his arms held her firmly against him. He rubbed one hand gently up and down her back and occasionally placed soft kisses against her tangled hair. And although she must have been a pure disaster in sight, she felt better than she had in ages. She snuggled into the lee of his neck, taking in his scent. It smelled of earth and dominance. She lowered her hand past the confines of his pants and circled his cock with her palm. Gently, she stroked his length as a sign of her new-found submission. In his embrace, for the first time since leaving Lazar, Cinder had indeed found that harem girl lost in the desert.

27

Cinder awoke from her nap feeling much better. The mental toll of the discipline far exceeded the small ache still present on her ass. The release had been much needed, and she actually felt lighter, as if a huge burden had been released. Everything had seemed to be spiraling out of control, and although her circumstances hadn't changed, she knew she had to face them differently. She no longer wanted to be the damsel in distress. She didn't want to be the fragile little girl everyone had to protect. Donte was right with what he'd said, she *was* a survivor, and that made her a fighter.

Getting out of bed, she decided to find him and tell him she no longer needed to be sheltered— that she could join the rest of the harem. As she entered the other room, she once again found no signs of Donte, but she could hear muffled voices on the other side of the door. With curiosity getting the better of her, she tiptoed over to it and pressed her ear against the wood.

She instantly recognized Donte's voice, and a commander. But there seemed to be another in the mix.

"We forged an alliance with the Salex commune, as well as the Lorince commune. Both will cost Lazar, with having to provide much needed supplies, but they have soldiers ready to fight. Both communes seem to have been preparing for this for some time. I would have to say they are the most experienced we have yet to see. Their soldiers are about five days away," said a voice that Cinder didn't recognize. "They have agreed to join forces and end Jaden's regime. Jaden is growing every day and are ruthless in their conquering of other communes. Jaden has made many enemies."

"That's good news," Donte said. "My men and I have been preparing the troops that trickle in, as well as the harem."

"The harem?" the commander asked. "How's that coming?"

"Slowly," Donte confessed. "But Nico assures us they'll be ready when the time comes."

"There's good news on horizon. There's word of

weather to the east. I've yet to confirm it, but have spoken to many who can," the commander said.

"Rain?" Donte asked.

"Possibly. We may see it before the battle. But if we're not successful—"

"We'll be successful, Commander. Jaden may be ruthless, but we have the numbers, especially with all the allied forces showing up daily," Donte interrupted.

"But if we're not," the commander continued on, "there is hope of possibly rebuilding elsewhere. Casen doesn't have the necessary resources. It's clear to see that with all the allied forces coming, our commune is already drying up."

"That's true. But I have no doubt that Lazar will be ours once again," Donte said. "Now, if you would please excuse me, I want to check on Cinder."

She quickly walked away from the door and sat down at the table. She was fidgeting with her fingers as he walked in the room.

"The conversation you were listening to brought good news," Donte said with a wicked smile.

"I... uh, I didn't mean to—"

"Eavesdrop?" he interrupted. How he could know amazed her.

Cinder's already sore ass throbbed at the

thought of what he would do. "I'm sorry," she offered.

Donte smiled again, walked to the chair across from her and sat down. "Did you sleep well?"

"Yes." She took a deep, calming breath. "I actually feel much better... stronger. I think I can rejoin the rest of the harem now."

Donte leaned back in his chair and crossed his arms. "Is that what you want?"

"Well, I don't want to be your burden any longer."

"Is that what you think you are to me?"

"Well, I... uh." Cinder looked down at the ground and then back up to meet his eyes. "I don't know what to think."

"Do *you* want to go back to the rest of the harem girls?" Donte asked again.

"No, not really. I just don't want to be in your way."

He smiled. "Enough of this talk. I would like you to stay with me, and you are not a burden. Don't say those words again or there will be consequences. I don't like it when you talk poorly of yourself." Changing the subject, Donte continued, "Tell me more about you, Cinder. I noticed on your upper back that you have a marking. What is it?"

She was surprised by his question. She hadn't

thought of the branding on her back for quite some time. It wasn't something she had to look at, and she tried her best to shut that part of her life out. The branding represented her past—it represented her birth commune Briar.

"It's a B with two lines underneath. The two lines are to represent the river that dried up many decades ago," she explained. "The B represents my birth commune, Briar. They branded all residents of the commune with the same mark."

"Other than your grandmother, did you have family? Are there people you miss?"

Cinder shook her head. "I miss no one. It's something I have learned to do in this ruthless world of ours. Life at Briar was not something I ever look back on. It's why the Palace of Lazar means so much to me. It was my only home. It's all I ever choose to know. My only past is the palace, and I choose to look no further than that in my memories."

Donte reached for two cups and a medium-sized container. He began to scoop its contents into the cups, then stood in silence while waiting for the water to bubble. When it did, he poured the water into the cups and brought them to the table.

"Did you build the Palace of Lazar?"

He smiled before taking a drink of his tea. "No.

My great-grandfather did. I simply rule what was left for me."

Cinder took a drink of her own tea. "Why were you building Casen? Weren't you happy with Lazar?"

"I'm trying to be proactive when it comes to resources. It's just a matter of time until everything withers away."

"Unless you find rain," Cinder interjected. "I heard one of your commanders mention rain."

Donte flashed that smile again; the one Cinder was growing to love. "Yes, rain. A myth to many, but I have hope that we'll see it someday."

"Do you think rain exists? I thought the clouds stopped producing moisture years and years ago."

He nodded. "That's true. But if we don't have hope of future survival, then what is the point of surviving now?"

She took another sip of her tea and asked, "Do you really think we will win back the palace?"

"Yes." The simple word spoken had so much power and conviction behind it. "But today is supposed to be a day of rest, not worry." He stood up and lifted her from his chair. "We'll end this conversation with my vow to you. I swear I will give you your past back. Lazar will be ours once again, and you will have a home to return to."

She looked up into his severe stare. Their lips

were so close, and she could almost feel a hum of electricity between them. She had been schooled in submission, though at times she'd not always been the best student. She had learned obedience, and had come close to mastering the art of femininity. But what she still lacked was knowledge on how to contain her emotions, how to hide her desire, and how to process this ever-growing love for the man who stood beside her.

She had been taught the art of surrender, but not the art of love.

Cinder closed her eyes and released a heavy sigh. When she opened them again, Donte leaned down and placed a soft kiss on her lips. He pulled away just enough to stare into her eyes and then kissed her again, this time with more force, with more passion, and with hunger.

Nothing was as sweet as the kiss he gave, nothing so intoxicating.

Cinder had never felt so drunk in love. This man who was capturing her mouth had also captured her heart. What she'd once defined as the feeling of safety, was actually the feeling of falling madly in love with her savior.

28

After the day of rest, the women had resumed their training bright and early the next morning. Elbi was there, but there was no sign of Mistress Tula. Cinder was dying to know what had happened, but hadn't had a chance to speak to Elbi yet. She anxiously awaited their first break for the day. She did her best to busy her mind with the training at hand. The words spoken by Donte still rang in her ears; 'we will make a warrior of you,' and she didn't want to let him down. Yes, a warrior she would be.

Today was a milestone for the women of the harem. After days of learning how to break free from holds, how to punch, kick and perform other examples of hand-to-hand combat, it was finally time to learn how to use a weapon.

Nico marched back and forth in front of the lined up women with each weapon in turn. He explained the pros and cons of each one. He compared choosing a weapon to choosing a lover. It was all about what *feels* right. After a schooling of all the weapons, he allowed each woman and her trainer the freedom to choose which one they wanted to use.

Cinder went straight to the sword. It seemed the most powerful and, she assumed, the easiest to learn. But when she picked it up, she realized it was a lot heavier than it looked. The idea of crossing the desert with the weight of the sword seemed daunting. She decided to choose something else. Looking over at Elbi, she could see that her friend had chosen a bow and arrow. That seemed fitting for Elbi, somehow. The next weapon she looked at was the battle axe. The fact that she couldn't even lift it made that decision quite easy. Finally, a cluster of throwing knives caught her eye. Light but deadly, and the handles of each had an intricate carving that exuded beauty. Yes, they felt right. She looked up at her trainer for confirmation, which was given by his smile and simple nod. Throwing knives it would be.

The next several hours were spent on learning how to properly hold, aim, and throw the knives. To Cinder's surprise, she was actually pretty good at it. Even Nico stopped and observed for some time, and then complimented her aim before he walked away. Just as one of the knives she threw hit the bull's eye, a much needed break was called.

Elbi must had been just as anxious to speak with Cinder, because she rushed over and said, "Are you doing all right after what happened the other day?" Cinder wiped the sweat off her brow as they walked away from everyone so they could talk.

She nodded. "Yes, but what about you? You're the one who got the worst of it."

"I'm fine. I applied some sort of ointment, and I feel a lot better. Okay... actually, the commander applied it." Elbi smiled at the memory. "To be honest with you, I enjoyed the extra pampering I received from him that night."

Cinder giggled. "My night wasn't so bad, either."

Elbi gasped and covered her mouth with her hand. "Oh my! So you belong to Prince Donte now?"

Cinder shrugged. "I suppose so. It's hard to say. All the harem rules and customs seem to have been thrown right out the window now. I don't know about anything anymore."

Elbi nodded. "I often think about what will happen if we do get the palace back. Everything is different. *We* are different."

"Do you think you'll join the harem again? Or do you think you will only belong to the commander?"

Elbi smiled. "I only belong to him. What that means in the palace, I'm not sure. But I know we'll figure it out together." Her smile grew even bigger. "He speaks of wanting children." She paused, her smile faded, and she looked at Cinder with a serious expression. "It's hard to fantasize of love when we're training to kill and about to go to war."

Cinder sighed. "I know. I'm trying to become that fighter, but I'm just not certain that I can." She took a deep breath. "I overheard Donte and the commanders talking."

Elbi nodded solemnly. "I often do, as well. It terrifies me. Even news that is supposed to be good is still terrifying. We're caught in this nightmare, and I just want out."

"They spoke of rain."

"I know." Elbi's voice sounded so fragile.

"Why does that make you sad? Is that what has been bothering you? I don't understand."

"It makes me sad that something that should be news of celebration is actually news of even more impending wars. Men will fight for those areas— the ones with rain—with even more vengeance than our precious Lazar commune. I hate hearing about it. I hate hearing all the plotting, all the closed-door secrets, all the plans to kill. I hate what we all are." Elbi sighed loudly. "I guess I've been upset, because I wish we didn't have to have victims to be victorious."

Silence sat between them as Elbi's words sunk in.

Elbi was silent for a few moments. Then she took a deep breath and asked, "Did you hear what happened to Mistress Tula? Or I guess I should say... Tula." It was obvious that she wanted to change the subject and the tone of the conversation.

"What? Tula?"

Elbi smiled. "Prince Donte was so angry with her about what she did to us that he punished her. But then it gets even better! The prince stripped her of her Mistress title. She is just Tula now, and is expected to train and be treated no differently than the rest of us. He also gave a strict warning to the other two sisters to never get overzealous in overseeing the harem again."

"Really? I can't believe he did that!" Cinder wasn't saddened by the news. Mistress Tula was far from a leader or someone they should have to respect. A sadist, yes, but a leader, no. "How did Donte punish her?"

Elbi laughed. "How do you think? This *is* Donte we are speaking of."

Donte's voice boomed over the courtyard. "Cinder, Elbi, can you follow us?"

Cinder turned to see Donte and the commander standing near the main building. She looked to Elbi for explanation, but when Elbi simply shrugged, they both walked toward the men.

When they approached, the commander placed his hand on Elbi's lower back and led the way to the main building. Donte reached for Cinder's hand and followed. Cinder swallowed back her fear. She scanned her memories for anything that could have gotten her and Elbi into trouble. Did Mistress Tula say something? Did she make up lies to get herself out of trouble?

As they entered the living quarters, Cinder was surprised to see Mistress Tula—Tula— waiting in the middle of the room. She looked nervous... even humble.

Donte was the first to speak. "I brought you girls in here so that Tula can rectify the incident that occurred."

Tula looked down at the ground and took a deep breath before steadying her shoulders and staring Cinder directly in the eyes. "I apologize, Cinder, for my behavior and treatment of you yesterday." She then looked at Elbi. "Elbi, I should have never punished you so severely."

Donte cleared his throat.

"I should not have punished you at all," Tula clarified. "I hope you both can forgive me."

"Tula was whipped in the same manner in which she whipped Elbi yesterday," Donte explained to Cinder. "Elbi was able to observe the punishment. She is no longer *Mistress* Tula, at least until she can prove her leadership abilities once again."

"But she still has one more punishment in store," the commander added. "And we'll allow both of you girls to administer it."

"Bare your ass," Donte commanded Tula.

She quickly did as he asked and bent over the back of a chair. She clearly knew what was to happen. Cinder could see the leftover signs of her punishment criss-crossed across the globes of her backside.

Donte pulled out an anal plug and a jar of lube from his pocket and handed them to Cinder. "Place the plug in her. Tula knows she is to wear it for the remainder of the day and must join the rest of the harem for training." He looked at Elbi. "You can help in whatever way you choose, as well."

Cinder froze, not sure she even wanted to do this. But then the excitement of the idea of finally giving Tula a taste of her own medicine won over. She tightened her hold on the butt plug and lube and walked over to the bent over Tula with Elbi right beside her. She could only imagine the anxiety, and humiliation that Tula must be feeling right about now, and Cinder was loving every moment of it. She handed the lube to Elbi to hold so she could smear some on the plug. Elbi bit her smiling lip, clearly holding back the laugh that threatened to escape. Cinder didn't make eye contact with Elbi because she knew it would lead to a fit of giggles.

"Bend over a little more, and spread your legs wider." The firmness in her voice surprised her. Cinder had never spoken to anyone with such command before.

Tula did as she asked, giving easier access to her anus. Cinder walked up, spread the woman's cheeks with Elbi's assistance and placed the plug right at the rosette. She pressed it in, but stopped just as Tula's hole was beginning to allow entrance. Cinder held the plug there, knowing that Tula wanted it just to go in at that moment and be done with it. Having it rest on the puckered flesh, spreading the most sensitive of entrances, added to the punishment. Cinder decided to move the plug from side to side and up and down, further stretching Tula's anus.

When Tula gasped and clenched, Cinder could only smile. Finally, Cinder allowed the plug to go all the way in, but then she pulled it all the way out and repeated the process all over again. Tula huffed and moaned with each motion. Cinder decided that Tula needed a little ass fucking herself, and happily did so.

After enough time had gone by, Cinder finally pushed the plug all the way in. Elbi released her butt cheeks, and Tula was left alone with her tender anus and full ass. Cinder walked away feeling a sense of strength. A little bit of sadist blended with her submissiveness, and she liked it... a lot. Maybe a little too much. She looked at Donte and felt a sense of pride when she saw his smile. He gave her a small nod, acknowledging that she had taken control. The lesson today; she had the power to master if she so chose.

29

Cinder stared at the contours of her nude body in the full-length mirror. In the past, some would have called her waifish, fragile, and slight. But now she looked on with pride. After weeks of daily training, her body had become muscular, lean, and even better... strong. And along with her growing physique came skill. She truly was becoming the warrior Donte wanted her to be. She had learned to use a sword—begrudgingly—but she had truly mastered the art of knife throwing. Even Nico said he had never seen such precision on hitting the target. Her days were filled with pride of her accomplishments.

Each day more and more reinforcements arrived. Casen was quickly outgrowing the space. Cinder had heard murmurings between Donte, the commanders and other soldiers about planning the attack on Jaden soon. There had been a time that Cinder would have been terrified to hear such news, but now she stood ready. She wanted to help take back the palace she so desperately loved. At the same time, she didn't want the old life she'd once lived. She had yet to figure out what would happen if they did return. What did that mean for her and Donte? Would they still reside in the same quarters? Was there a future for them?

So many questions and no answers.

Not even a hint from Donte as to what he was thinking or wanting. The only thing she did know was love. She loved the Prince of Lazar... was in love with him. Of that much she could be certain.

Cinder had noticed that as the weeks went by, she had seen less of Donte. Both were gone all day and when they returned to the quarters, they were extremely exhausted from the day's events and sleep was all either craved. When she awoke in the morning, Donte was always long gone. They each had their duties, and for the first time in Cinder's life, she was thriving. She had been given a gift: the gift of strength.

The sound of footsteps entering the room snapped her from her thoughts. "It is a beautiful sight," Donte said as he walked up behind her. "Your body represents hard work, dedication, and fortitude." He placed a kiss on her shoulder, then continued to kiss up her neck and nibbled on her ear.

The Cinder of the past would have been embarrassed at being caught staring at her naked body. But the woman of today felt pride. She had grown stronger every day through blood, sweat and most certainly tears.

She turned around, wrapped her arms around his neck and placed a soft kiss to his lips. "I even have muscles on my inner thighs." She giggled and kissed him again. "I think I can thank *you* for that."

Donte smiled against another kiss. "I plan to maintain those muscles long after we have reclaimed Lazar." He tightened his grip on her hips and kneeled before her. "I enjoy the muscles very much."

He began to place soft kisses along her inner thigh, slowly working his way up to her sex. Kiss by kiss, breath by breath, he snaked his way to his final destination. Licking up one pussy lip and back down the other, he moaned against her.

Cinder gasped and reached down to curl her fingers in his untamed hair. "Donte," she panted. She flung her head back and closed her eyes as he continued to lick, thrusting his tongue deeper into her pussy.

"Mmm, so wet for your prince."

Cinder's heart skipped. "Yes... so wet. I need my prince's cock—"

A loud knock on the door broke the erotic spell. Donte shot up and headed to the main room, and Cinder scrambled for her clothes. The knock pounded again, followed by, "Donte, open up. Jaden is approaching!"

When Cinder joined Donte in the front room, she saw Donte, the commanders, Nico and a few other soldiers engaged in a heated discussion.

"The scout said they are about five miles out," Nico announced.

"I think we should head them off before they get to Casen," a commander suggested.

Another commander shook his head. "We're stronger here. We have defenses and are prepared."

"And what if they are victorious? Then they succeeded at capturing our only other commune," Donte countered. He turned to Nico. "Did the scout say how many?"

"Hundreds. They are definitely coming with the intent of conquering," he answered. "But that's good news for us. If we are victorious, we can storm Lazar when Jaden is at its weakest."

"Exactly," Donte agreed. "That should be our plan. Fight now and win, and then counterattack as quickly as we can. Before they can build reinforcements."

A commander turned to one of the soldiers. "Prepare the men for battle."

"Gather the women and secure them in the main building," Donte ordered Nico. "I want several men surrounding them at all times."

"Wait!" Cinder interjected. Everyone turned, noticing her standing in the room for the first time. "We can fight as well. We're ready."

Donte shot her a stern look. His face made it quite clear that he didn't like his directive to be questioned.

Cinder continued, "We can't help if we're locked away."

"We'll be fine with the men we have," Donte said, with Nico nodding in agreement.

"But what about the women you have? We have been training daily for over a month. Elbi can shoot a bow better than anyone. Nico said himself that my aim is precise. And the rest of the women all have their own talents. Isn't this what we have been training for?" Cinder wasn't going to back down. Even though she was trying to sound courageous, she was avoiding Donte's stare. The daggers coming from his eyes were more lethal than any knife she could throw. She looked at Nico for some kind of reinforcement. "Nico? Are we not soldiers?"

Nico looked at her, to the men, and then back

at her. He didn't respond at first, and seemed angry for even being put in this position. Finally, he turned back to the men. "I believe that Jaden will be looking for the harem. Killing the entire harem will send a powerful message. I think the best thing would be to disperse the women amongst all the soldiers. Have them fight, rather than be sitting ducks in one space."

Nico's answer wasn't exactly the support Cinder was looking for, but at least he was agreeing the harem shouldn't all be locked in a room waiting to see if they would die or not. Thankfully, he was allowing each woman to take her own fate into her own hands.

"Very well," Donte spat out.

Donte nodded, as did the commanders. "Prepare for battle."

Cinder was about to follow everyone out of the house when Donte grabbed her by the arm and pulled her back. The fury on his face seemed more daunting than the battle about to happen.

He pulled her so close to his face that she could almost feel the heat from his anger. "Never," he growled. "Never question me in front of others."

She squared her shoulders, swallowed back her fear, and stared directly into his eyes. "Then *never* question my ability."

Donte remained quiet, but his face softened, as did his tight grip on her arm.

"I'm not the same woman I once was, Donte. Let me prove to you that I can be that warrior you believed I could be."

"I know how strong you are. You have no need to prove anything to me. What you do not understand is that the thought of you in battle makes *me* afraid."

"Because I'm not strong enough?"

"No. Because I love you. Because I don't want the woman I love to die by the blade of a sword."

His words punched at her gut and stole her breath. He had declared his love. Prince Donte of Lazar loved her. She'd known he cared for her, had sexual desires for her, and wanted her to be near him. But she hadn't been sure that love was anything he felt.

Tears clouded her eyes as she whispered, "And I love you."

"Then allow me to protect you. Allow me to keep you safe. I could not live with myself if you were killed."

"How? By hiding in a hole somewhere, shaking in fear of the unknown? Should I have another panic attack while I wait to see if someone comes to murder me? Should I cry? Should I break down and fall to my knees?" Cinder took a few steps back and asked, "Is that the woman you love?"

He walked toward her, closing the distance between them once more. "That's not the woman you are."

"Exactly! What you don't realize is that you gave me the greatest gift I could ever ask for. You gave me the ability to fight. You healed the beaten soul inside of me. You made me realize that I can do this." Tears threatened to fall, but Cinder refused to let them. "Please don't take that gift away."

Donte nodded, looking sad. He then cleared his throat and his expression grew firm. "You'll do as I command. You'll fight where I say, and stay near me. I'm one of the commanders of this army, and you are a soldier. You'll follow my commands and never question. It is your duty as a soldier in this army to do so. Do you understand?"

Cinder smiled. "Yes, sir."

Donte gave her a weak smile in return. "Then let us prepare for battle."

30

Can anyone ever be ready for battle? Cinder pondered that question as she stood in position, fingering the heavy bag of throwing knives at her side. Her other side was weighed down by the sword she was forced to carry, even though she hated to do so. Donte had told her to stand ready by one of the entrances. He told her that once the door was breached, to throw the knives and aim at their eyes. She'd also been instructed to remain behind the protective wall, and not to engage in hand-to-hand unless absolutely necessary. He then kissed her softly and left. Cinder hadn't seen him since, but she had no doubt he was nearby.

She stood there for what felt like an eternity. Waiting. Waiting for Jaden. She looked around and watched the hundreds of soldiers waiting as well, worry obvious on their faces although none would speak of it. With all the soldiers ready for the attack, she could see no sign of Elbi or anyone else she knew, but she wasn't going to disobey Donte and leave her post to go searching.

Sweat trickled down her arm as the blazing sun began to set. Would Jaden wait until nightfall to attack? That seemed the most logical thing, but the waiting game tortured her. She tried to busy her mind and not allow it to go to thoughts of what it would be like to kill someone again. How would it feel to throw a knife and actually hit a human's eye? No... those thoughts could not exist right now. Those thoughts led to weakness.

"Cinder," she heard being whispered behind her. She turned quickly to see Elbi hunched down with her bow ready. "I wanted to tell you that I'll be in the tower behind me." Cinder looked over Elbi's shoulder at the tower looming over them. "I'll shoot anyone who tries to get near you."

She nodded, not sure what to say. The fear of what was happening began to weigh her down.

"I love you. You're going to be just fine. You can do this," Elbi assured her. She then turned and quickly made her way to her post, leaving Cinder to struggle with her internal demons and fighting back the fear that made her want to run and search for Donte.

Just as the shadows were taking over, the calls of war pierced the air. Shouts, screams, commands... even the first groans of death. What was once a stagnant silence became wave after wave of chaos.

Cinder held her hand on the hilt of her sword and palmed a knife with the other. She waited with the sounds of war all around the outside of the encampment. She waited for the doors to be opened as fear threatened to paralyze her body. So far, the walls of Casen were holding Jaden back. No one had entered, and the damage was being done to Jaden on the other side by the archers.

The question of whether she would see battle was answered by a loud crash, followed by what was left of Jaden's men storming through. It was her time to perform. Without any hesitation, she began to throw one knife after another, aiming for their eyes. Moving targets were harder, but her intentions were met for the most part. Arrows whirled around her, swords clanging against swords. People cried out in agony as weapons made contact with flesh. But Cinder focused on her knives and her duty. A tidal wave of mayhem surrounded her, with its only saving grace being that it didn't give Cinder time to think. It didn't give her time to process that she was engaged in battle. She did not have a second to consider that people were dying all around her as bloodshed became the norm.

As the knives were becoming few, the bodies surging forward slowed. The sounds of misery lessened, the howls of the night weakened, and after a time of nightmarish proportions, the fight seemed to end. Cinder stopped throwing and stood. Silence...

And then the cheers of victory roared through Casen.

Had they won?

Was that it?

Was the attack from Jaden over?

Donte? Where was Donte? Cinder didn't know as she stood and circled in place, searching for the answer. Was he one of the fallen soldiers? No doubt he'd led his men, charging toward his own death in the hopes of victory. Was Donte dead?

A sound behind her brought the answer, Cinder turning on bare heel to lay her eyes upon a tall figure emerging from the shadows. Her heart skipped a beat as anticipation filled her, her breath catching in her throat as she waited to see if it would be her lover returning to her or just her mind playing some terrible farce against her.

His face was weary, and he had deep circles

beneath his dark eyes. He looked very much the tired man, the warrior. He looked broken, almost defeated. And yet, when their eyes met, the doubt that had filled his gaze, the fear, melted away.

Neither of them moved for what seemed an eternity, both believing the other to be a dream, a mirage conjured up by tired minds to soothe the tormented soul. He would be the first to break that silent stillness that seemed to encompass them like a heavy blanket.

"Cinder!" she heard called from the distance. Her name bubbled from his lips like the most precious of secrets. She smiled to see Donte charging forward, his lengthy stride closing the distance between them. She remained in position, as he had commanded, until she was engulfed in his arms and spun in a circle. "We won. It's over."

Cinder knew they both had waited with building anxiety for the battle to end, both having their own hopes as to the outcome. By the end, each had only wished it over, if just to see the other's face once more. As brutal minutes had passed and turned into hours of murder, fear planting a seed of doubt within their hearts, both had feared the other dead.

She didn't speak, but the joy she felt shimmered in her brown eyes, spilling down her cheeks in crystal droplets, soon to be wiped away by dirty fingers of his calloused hands.

"I thought I had lost you. It was my biggest fear through this all." Her voice was barely a whisper above the gentle breeze that blew her hair over one cheek. She gripped at what remained of his tattered shirt, fingertips smoothing over his sun-kissed flesh.

"I wasn't going to die this way. Not by Jaden. Our story has just begun and I wasn't going to cut it short." His fingers, stained with blood and dirt, slid over her cheek as his lips met hers in the tenderest of kisses. Passionate, fulfilling, perfect.

The pain of war, of loss, of defeat... and now victory.

When finally their lips parted, there was nothing to be found between the pair but smiles and warmth, compassion and understanding passing through the depth of their gaze. His fingers wound into her hair, the strength of his arms crushing her into him as her tears soaked his chest.

"As much as I want to truly celebrate in other ways, we need to hurry. We need to leave for Lazar tonight. We need to strike now before Jaden can rebuild."

"Just allow me to stay with you," she pleaded with him, her fingers clutching desperately at his chest, fear once again gripping her. "I don't want to be apart again."

He merely shook his head, brushing her lips with his own before he took her hand, twining their fingers together. "Nothing will separate us again. This is a promise I will make."

"NICO IS LEADING the troops to Lazar now. We didn't want to waste a minute," a commander informed Donte as they stood in the main house.

Donte had a gash across his forehead but seemed fine otherwise. Elbi held her commander's hand as if she would never let it go, undoubtedly relieved to have the man she loved still alive. Cinder understood the feeling as she watched Donte. Not only had they won the battle; all the women of the harem had survived the attack. Though many soldiers had died, Cinder hadn't lost anyone she'd been close to, and she was grateful to be alive and well in the same room with the man she loved.

Donte nodded. "Good. Let us get everything and everyone ready for departure. We'll leave first thing in the morning. Let everyone rest for the journey. Hopefully by the time we arrive, the Palace of Lazar will be ours once again." Donte smiled at Cinder and squeezed the hand he hadn't released since they'd been reunited.

"What about Casen?" Elbi asked.

"We're handing it over to the allied forces. It's our gift to them for all their help in defeating Jaden," Donte answered.

The commander nodded and added, "The reign of Jaden is not over yet. We'll need the continued help from our allies in order to keep Jaden at bay. Giving away Casen is our first step toward peace. Greed leads to war, and we plan to share our wealth."

"Today we won. In a few days, with Jaden being weak, we will regain Lazar. But Jaden will try to rebound, and we must be ready." Donte's voice deepened as he spoke, and his face grew dark.

"And we will be ready. We will reclaim the Palace of Lazar and never lose it again," the commander said.

Donte's jaw tightened and he nodded. "When Jaden comes knocking again, we will answer the door with vengeance."

31

Deep in the desert, the clash of swords and shrill screams could be heard for miles as the harem marched toward the palace. A war had broken out two weeks ago, and when Nico and the troops came swiftly down the dunes, they attacked Jaden with a ferocity that would become legend for hundreds of years.

Now, as they approached what was once their beautiful palace, Cinder stopped and clutched her heart.

"I see it," she declared, her voice raspy from the days of travel through the harsh desert.

Other gasps and cries were heard as each person glimpsed what she observed. Their palace stood—though battered—it stood free from Jaden. Charred land, burnt structures, and smoldering fires still lingered, but there was not a Jaden soldier in sight.

Nico came charging up the dunes on horseback with pride in his eyes. Behind him rode several more men. One man had a stake in his hands, with the head of General Rhys impaled on it. The general's eyes remained wide open, his face frozen in the fear he'd felt right before someone had ended his life and beheaded him. Flies had already begun feasting on his dead flesh. General Rhys was dead. Cinder could barely take her eyes off the head of a man who had tormented so many.

It took all of her will to look at Nico as he approached and declared, "We have conquered the Palace of Lazar! It's ours! The Palace of Lazar is ours!"

32

The Commander stood up to begin the celebration. He proudly held up a wine glass and bellowed, "My friends, my family, I am honored to stand before you. We sit here and celebrate in our precious Palace of Lazar. What we once lost, we have found again. What we may have once taken for granted, we now see as a prized jewel." His gaze went to Elbi. "And some of us have found the most precious gift of all—love." Everyone in the room cheered in unison when the commander went to one knee. "Will you, my dear Elbi, do me the honor of being my wife?"

"Yes, yes," Elbi answered, as tears streamed down her face. "I will marry you!"

Cheers erupted again and congratulations rang out. Cinder smiled and nodded at all the toasts.

Although she was delighted for her best friend, seeing such complete love struck her to the core with jealousy. She tried to hide her unwelcome emotions, but tears threatened to fall. Donte must have sensed her discomfort, because he reached for her hand. A soft squeeze from his fingers did wonders for her rampant emotions.

"So tonight," Donte announced, standing up to add to the toast, "we celebrate our victories. Tomorrow, we rebuild. The palace is not what it once was. In fact, it's badly beaten. But the shambles are ours, and we will make it thrive once again." More cheers broke out as Donte returned to his seat, clenching tightly the hand of Cinder.

For the next hour, everyone launched into playful banter, and Cinder found herself laughing more now than she ever had. She'd almost forgotten what it was like to laugh so easily. Fear was replaced with joy, war was replaced with friendship, and death was replaced with promise of the future.

Just as Cinder was getting ready to call it a night, and wondering where she would sleep that evening, Donte wrapped his arm around her and leaned forward so his lips were at her ear.

"Do you mind taking a walk with me?" he asked quietly.

The heat of his breath against her skin sent a

shiver down her spine and her insides heated almost instantly. She smiled and nodded, trying to keep her composure. Donte stood and helped her out of her seat, and they slipped out of the dining room without anyone saying anything or noticing.

"Where are we going?" she asked, when Donte took her hand and started pulling her down the hallway.

"Home," he said in a whisper, urging her to follow him, pulling her into a room.

The room they were standing in once held a lavish bed with four posts, with a canopy stretched over it. The walls were once decorated with opulent paintings, and ornate rugs once adorned the marble floors. The elaborate room that was once Donte's had been plundered, and nothing endured the possession of Jaden. All that remained was a mattress with some simple bedding.

"This will be our new quarters. It's not much now, but I will focus my attentions on bringing back the glory that you deserve," he said, gesturing to his room with a sweep of his arm.

"Our quarters?" she asked. They hadn't discussed this, and Cinder realized that she had desperately hoped that Donte would still want to live with her even after they returned to the palace.

"Of course, Cinder. I can't imagine spending even one night apart from you."

With her heartbeat piercing her chest, she walked up to him and placed her forehead against his body. "That makes me so very happy to hear."

"Here, let us lie down on *our* bed," he said softly, leading her to the mattress on the floor. He fell back against the pillows at the head of the bed and she joined him, leaning her head against his chest.

Donte smelled like security, if there was such a smell to describe it, and she inhaled deeply as she nuzzled her face into the lee of his neck. His warm embrace made her feel as if she were sinking into his body. She felt heavy in love. She took another deep breath and released it slowly, taking in the moment of complete relaxation.

"I've been waiting for this day for so long," he murmured against the top of her head, his fingers stroking her scalp. "I've wanted nothing more than to hold you in my arms, in our home—the palace."

She simply nodded.

"What is it you want of the future, Cinder?"

She froze.

He must have felt her tension. "Why does the question bother you?"

"I don't know how you want me to answer it." She held her breath, not sure what to say or what to do.

"The truth. I simply ask the truth of you."

"I want love," she confessed.

"Do you not feel love?" he asked, as he continued petting her hair.

There was a long moment of silence. Cinder glanced up at him and before she could give him an answer, Donte's lips were pressed against hers, and her body caught aflame. She smiled against the kiss and let her hands wander up to stroke his face. Reveling in the taste of his lips, she softly moaned with the need for more.

"I love you," he whispered against the kiss. "I love you more than I ever thought possible. The love I have for you I fear will suffocate you with the intensity."

"And I love you," she admitted freely.

"I don't know what tomorrow will bring when it comes to the palace, but I do know that from this day on, I want you by my side."

"What about the harem?" She didn't want to ask the question, because she feared the answer. She didn't want to go back. She didn't want anyone of the harem to pleasure Donte. She wanted conventional, but feared he did not.

"The harem will serve its original purpose. We will not take away from what the harem is, what it stands for, and what it will become." He kissed her softly before continuing. "But you will no longer be part of the harem, and I have no need for it either. The harem will simply be the jewels to this broken palace. You'll serve me as the harem once did. And I'll serve you."

"Will you not miss the harem?"

Donte smiled. "The harem gave me beauty. I now have this with you. The harem gave me surrender. This I will still demand from you. The harem gave me sex. And this, my dear Cinder, you have mastered. The harem offers me nothing I do not already hold with you."

She blushed with the memory of their sexual experiences.

He kissed her deeply, forcing his tongue into her mouth only to be met with her carnal return. He rolled her onto her back in one swift move, never breaking the kiss. He effortlessly removed her silk, exposing her body to him, and then quickly shed his own. His eyes locked with hers, casting a spell of seduction. She knew what was to come, but the anticipation nearly choked her.

"Can you leave the harem and only belong to me?" he asked as he straddled her now nude body. His cock stood hard and ready, and Cinder could not keep her eyes from it. "I can be very demanding in all ways. Your time, your attention, your presence."

"I only belong to you," she panted, licking her lips in anticipation of his dick entering her mouth.

He lowered himself and kneeled before her

face, his cock mere inches from her lips. "Can you surrender to me?" He placed the tip of his penis on her lips. "I will require a lot. I can already tell my thirst for you will only grow with each day."

"My submission is yours," she answered, and licked the shiny pre cum that escaped his ready sex.

With a growl that rose from the depths of his chest, Donte thrust his dick into her expecting mouth. She took the girth and began to suck with a hunger, a need, an uncontrollable urge to give the man she loved pleasure. Up and down as she closed her mouth even tighter with every move. Up and down as she moaned against his flesh, reverberating against the mass that filled her mouth. Donte grabbed her by the hair and helped guide her head, claiming his will.

He quickly pulled out and flipped her over, positioning her on all fours. "I can't be gentle," he hissed as he slapped her ass.

Cinder moaned at the sting of his hand, hungry for more. "And that is not what I ask. Spank my ass, Donte. Show me who my master is! Spank me, and show me what will happen if I disobey you. Show me, Donte. Show me, please."

As if she had just released the dam, Donte began the intoxicating punishment. Spank after spank, his hand descended against her milky surface. With each searing smack, her flesh sparked. She held her position and squeezed her eyes against the sting, the pain, and against the most intense pleasure. Signs of her arousal dripped down her pussy to coat her inner thighs as she pleaded for more. He continued to spank without mercy or without letting up. The force of each swat of her ass rocked her body forward, only to have her thrust her ass back, eagerly awaiting the next punishing blow.

He rewarded her surrender to his discipline by thrusting his cock into her pussy. Not gentle, not with ease, but with a capturing onslaught. He dominated; he took and captured her body. Her orgasm exploded around his cock as her screams lined the room, only to be followed by his moans of release. Nothing, nothing, nothing could compare to the impression left on her soul. To be mastered. To be conquered. To be *his*!

"Do you hear that?" Donte asked as they lay in each other's arms. He sat up and listened. Cinder sat up as well and tried to focus her attention on the noise around her. She tried to keep the panic at bay.

"Is it Jaden? Are they attacking?" Her voice

cracked, revealing the terror that came storming in.

"No." Donte got out of bed and quickly got dressed. He threw Cinder's silk to her. A rumble shook the outside, followed by another. "Hear that?"

Cinder quickly got dressed. "Oh god! It's Jaden!"

Donte smiled when the rumble happened again. "No, my love. I believe it's thunder! I believe it's signaling a storm. Hurry and get dressed."

They rushed outside and joined everyone else from the celebratory dinner. They, too, had heard the noise and had come rushing outdoors to see for themselves.

"Thunder!" Nico confirmed, when he turned to see Donte and Cinder running outside. A bolt of lightning shot across the blackness.

And then it happened. The sky up above opened up and drops of water emerged. Cinder turned her face toward the sky and felt the rain fall upon her desert-worn skin. Drop after drop of water came pouring out of the night, splattering onto the withered and cracked ground below.

"Rain! It's rain," came shouts from everyone around. Cries, cheers, and laughter blended with the booming cadence of the storm. Drops turned to sheets of water as the sky unleashed the storm.

Cinder turned to Donte who also had his face turned up toward the sky, allowing the rain to drench his body. She watched as members of the harem began to dance around, their silks wet against their skin. She looked over to see Elbi and the commander embracing, kissing with the rain falling all around. And then she turned completely and looked back at the Palace of Lazar. It stood in all its glory with the night sky as its backdrop. The rain began to wash away the scars Jaden had caused. The rain showered away signs of the war, washing away the soot, the filth, and the contamination of the evil that had once resided there. All that remained now was a palace being cleansed by Mother Nature herself. The rain offered a new beginning. It was their reward for their glory. They had conquered The Palace of Lazar—her home, her future, her love.

And They Lived Happily Ever After...

Do you want to hear about my new releases coming up?

Be sure to sign up for my VIP newsletter so you are the first to know when my next book is coming.

Alta's Newsletter

ABOUT THE AUTHOR

Alta Hensley is a USA TODAY bestselling author of hot, dark and dirty romance. She is also an Amazon Top 100 bestselling author. Being a multi-published author in the romance genre, Alta is known for her dark, gritty alpha heroes, sometimes sweet love stories, hot eroticism, and engaging tales of the constant struggle between dominance and submission.

Check out Alta Hensley:
Website: www.altahensley.com
Facebook: facebook.com/AltaHensleyAuthor
Twitter: twitter.com/AltaHensley
Instagram: instagram.com/altahensley
Amazon: amazon.com/Alta-Hensley
BookBub: bookbub.com/authors/alta-hensley
Sign up for Alta's Newsletter: readerlinks. com/l/727720/nl

For all of my books, check out my Amazon Page!

http://amzn.to/2CTmeen

Made in the USA
Las Vegas, NV
27 September 2022

56032243R00190